Merak and I went to a view room near the gym. I punched up Instructvid 56–40. The screen came back: "For Emergency Use Only." Then the screen locked up. We had to go through the whole clearance routine, like maybe this Instructvid was going to reveal the Q-wave secrets. I thought maybe I punched up the Instructvid for invasion by unknown aliens. I couldn't understand why all the security.

Then the naked vidguy appeared on the screen. It was the same naked vidguy who is on all the health-and-hygiene Instructvids. He's supposed to represent the average healthy human male. Except he doesn't look like a normal human male. He looks like a gung-ho cadet who has taken physconditioning four times running just for fun, and he's hung like a Denebulan stud. And he's always completely naked, even if it's the Instructvid on lowgrav toothbrushing.

Also by

LARS EIGHNER:
Whispered in the Dark
American Prelude
Bayou Boy
B.M.O.C.
Gay Cosmos

CLAY CALDWELL:
Stud Shorts
Tailpipe Trucker
Queers Like Us
All-Stud

QSFx2

QUEER SCIENCE FICTION

Lars Eighner and Clay Caldwell

Introduction by Aaron Travis

BADBOY

The stories in this volume are copyrighted © 1994 by their respective authors, Lars Eighner and Clay Caldwell.

Stories by Clay Caldwell: "A Dort Called Tiger" first appeared (as "Alien Sex Slave") in *Guys*, 1992, "Pro vs. Con" first appeared in *Drummer* issue 154, April 1992; "Renegade" first appeared in *Inches*, Jan. 1989, "Galac 19" first appeared in *Honcho Overload*, Feb. 1994; "Great State" first appeared in a Larry Townsend publication.

Stories by Lars Eighner: "Starhauler" first appeared in *Inches*, Feb. 1990; "The Desert Inn" first appeared in *Stallion*, Oct. 1992; "The Trade" first appeared in *Torso*; "Midnight Oil" first appeared in *Inches*, Sept. 1989; "October Moon" first appeared in *Advocate Men*, June 1990.

QSFx2
Copyright © 1995 by Lars Eighner and Clay Caldwell
Introduction © 1995 by Aaron Travis
All Rights Reserved

No part of this book may be reproduced, stored in a retrieval system, or transmitted in any form, by any means, including mechanical, electronic, photocopying, recording or otherwise, without prior written permission of the publishers.

First BADBOY Edition 1995

First Printing September 1995

ISBN 1-56333-278-7

Cover Photograph © 1995 Tara Striano

Cover Design by Dayna Navaro

Manufactured in the United States of America
Published by Masquerade Books, Inc.
801 Second Avenue
New York, N.Y. 10017

QSFx2

Introduction: Blast Off! by Aaron Travis   7

5 x Clay Caldwell

Great State   13

A Dort Called Tiger   45

Pro vs. Con   55

Renegade   67

Galac 19   77

5 x Lars Eighner

Starhauler   91

October Moon   111

Midnight Oil   123

The Desert Inn   135

The Trade   155

Introduction: Blast Off!

by Aaron Travis

Since the beginnings of the genre, there have been writers who make their careers writing science fiction—like H. G. Wells, whose fantastic novels fill entire shelves—and there have been writers who only dabble—like E. M. Forster, whose science fiction was limited to a story called "The Machine Stops." But "The Machine Stops" is a masterpiece and people still read it. Does that make Forster a science-fiction writer? Or does the fact that his enduring fame rests on some of the finest novels of the century, like *Howard's End* and *A Passage to India*, make him any less a science-fiction writer?

The whole idea of genre writing has always lent itself to such tortuous discussions, made all the more vexing when genres overlap—as when science fiction merges into erotica. The immensely prolific Clay

Caldwell is revered for his porno stories about horny truckers and hayseeds, but he's also written two futuristic novels originally published as porn paperbacks (now available again from Badboy), *All-Stud* (1969) and *Service Stud* (1978), as well as a handful of shorter science-fiction stories. These works are decidedly erotic and very much of a piece with Caldwell's other erotic writing, but they're also science fiction—so which shelf do you put them on?

Lars Eighner made a reputation for himself as a writer of remarkably crafted short stories about men and sex, selling his work to gay skin mags. Then he recounted his three years of homelessness and hitchhiking in the best-selling *Travels with Lizbeth* and became a darling of the literati. Along the way he's given us a handful of amazing stories in the realm of science fiction and fantasy. Is he a science fiction writer? A pornographer? A literary essayist?

Ultimately, of course, these distinctions matter only to academics and to those who market books. The ultimate judge of any writer is the consumer of his craft—the reader. This volume has been created for the reader who happens to like queer stuff *and* science fiction. Between its covers you'll find the complete shorter science fiction written to date by its two authors, neither of whom has created enough in the genre to make up a solo anthology.

The combination is more than convenient. Caldwell and Eighner provide fascinating points of similarity and contrast. Both, clearly, are concerned primarily with homosexual desire and arousal. But the uses they make of their fantastic devices are quite different.

Introduction

For Caldwell, a futuristic setting is simply one more way to explore the themes that fascinate him about sex between men—dominance and submission, rites of passage, cyclical hierarchies of power and maturity, self-discovery. He has explored the same themes in other settings, such as military barracks and boarding schools, but a fanciful all-male future allows him even more freedom to project his characters and their desires to logical extremes.

Eighner ventures beyond realism for a wider range of reasons, and each of his five stories in this collection is strikingly unique. "Starhauler" uses the isolation of space travel to show us adult men finding out about sex—real, man-to-man sex—for the first time. The setting allows Eighner to deal with sexual discovery in ways that a realistic story simply couldn't. "The Trade" trades on the familiar straight fear that gayness is communicable, takes the idea literally, turns it on its head, and pushes it to a disturbing conclusion. "October Moon" and "Midnight Oil" aren't science fiction, but stories of the spooky sort; I'll say nothing to give them away. "The Desert Inn" is a small masterpiece of sword and sorcery, exactly the kind of gory, lurid epic that I suspect Eighner's fellow Texan, Robert E. Howard (the creator of Conan the Barbarian), always wanted to write.

Enough! The future can't wait any longer—it's here. Strap yourself in, wet your finger (to turn the page...) and get ready to blast off!

5 x CLAY CALDWELL

Great State

At the end of the standard work session, the electronic tone sounded, and Dort joined the men hustling to the autotransit. He inserted his identity card in the acceptance slot, received it back and entered the cab, and he joked with his comrades about what they'd do during the rest interval as they were whisked to Residence 4708.

Once at the gleaming multistoried building, Dort used the lifter to reach his cubit, and once again his card opened the door. The room was large, and the walls were painted in cool State-approved colors. The furnishings were sparse and masculine, and Dort emptied his pockets automatically and began to undress.

The young man had wavy brown hair and strong clean-cut features. His bronzed physique was athletically muscled. A swirl of dark silk spun across the solid curves of his chest, a narrow trail descending to the wide thicket of pubic wire at his groin, and his cock fell loosely, its thickness almost hiding his free-hanging testicles.

Stripped, Dort bundled his clothing and dropped them into the cleaning chute, knowing they would be returned before the rest interval ended because each item bore an invisible computab showing his identity number. Great State offered the comrades every benefit.

Fingering his heavy genitals proudly, he sauntered to the hygiene alcove at the other side of the room. He was pleased at the size of his prick and the way it could swell up, longer and thicker, more than many he'd seen, and less than damn few.

Dort stepped into the plastishield. Seconds after he closed the door, the cleansing cycle began. A torrent of preset tepid water gushed down on him, flowing all over his husky physique. It stopped abruptly, giving him time to position himself with arms and legs spread. Then the second cycle started. Beams of lather aimed at the top of his head and moved downward from every side. When they reached his waist, they poured into the cleft in his ass and spanked against his genitals. He felt the usual tingling in his dick and grinned, remembering the times he had halted the machine at this point and jerked off. The sprays continued down his muscled thighs and legs to his feet. The rinsing commenced immediately, following the previous pattern rapidly. An instant later, a flash of heat dried him and refreshed his all-over tan, and the cleansing ended.

Freshly scrubbed, Dort left the plastishield. He took the shaving mask from its wall holder, and fit it carefully to his jaws. As the gentle pressure removed the stubble, he glanced at the suction cup hanging on the wall. When applied to any part of the body, it produced the sensations of a warm, hungry mouth. It even expanded to take a rigid cock if a man wanted a blowjob. Great State provided for all the comrade's needs.

"Not tonight," Dort muttered as he replaced the shaving mask. "I'm out for some real action."

Returning to the main room, he opened the clothing rack and selected what he called his "hunting uniform": a skintight shirt and trousers that outlined the masculine strength of his body. Once dressed, he downed two nourishment pills from the dispenser. Immediately the hunger was gone from his belly but not the hunger in his loins.

He knew he could cut loose with any of the men in the other cubits, or he could join the group sex combat in the dim-lit sports space. No, this was the night for the park!

He slipped his identity card into a rear pocket and left quickly, taking the lifter to street level and walking the short distance to the sprawling, wooded area.

Few knew or cared about the history of Impact Park, but some said it marked the site of a tremendous explosion before the Great State was established, which would account for the ruins. As a boy, Dort and the other Youth Trainees in his unit came to play and explore the broken remains of what might have been a factory or office center. When he reached manhood, he discovered that the area served a different purpose at night.

As he entered the park, Dort felt the familiar sex

excitement rise. Loafing down the main path, he could see night-lit figures in the bushes, some already locked together and others on the hunt, and he remembered the times he had connected with some stranger and gotten his rocks off under the stars.

Dort felt drawn to the tunneled entrance of the ruin. Immediately inside, he found two bare-chested men standing side by side, heads, down, hands locked behind their backs. One was tall and lean while the other was shorter and chunky. Both had their hair bristle-clipped like caps on their scalps. Dort knew they were Zedros, body-shaved and marked with an untanned strip at their hips, State-stationed to serve the comrades in any way ordered. He had used a Zedro at times, but it seemed as mechanical as using the suction tube in his cubit.

Another man came into the tunnel and stopped in front of the first Zedro. He opened his fly and hauled out his cock and balls.

"Take me off!" he said sharply. "I'm in a hurry."

The Zedro dropped to his knees obediently and took the offered prick in his mouth without looking up or bringing his hands forward to touch the man.

There was nothing unusual about watching a comrade get his rocks off, but Dort was interested in all-out action. He moved deeper into the shadows, viewing the men: no more Zedros, studs like himself eager for combat, some already coupled, none of them giving a State-approved damn about who might see them. He wasn't sure what he was looking for, and he went on to the rear of the corridor, slouching back against the wall near the doorway to the blackness he had never entered.

He waited. Then he saw a hulk of a man silhouetted at the entrance. Ignoring the Zedros and the others, the figure moved down the passage until he stopped in front of Dort, as if knowing he would be there.

Dort couldn't see the man's face in the dimness, but he felt hypnotized and unable to move. The stranger outlined the curves and hollows of Dort's torso with his fingers, then began unfastening the shirt.

In response, Dort raised his hands and found that the man's shirt was already spread open; he ran his hands over the hairy barrel chest.

"My name's Dort," he murmured, indicating his willingness to share sex combat.

The stranger answered with a grunt and wrapped both arms around Dort. Dort's dick pulsed full-hard in his pants as he embraced the burly male. The man pulled back slightly, still holding Dort in place with one arm, and he brought a capsule up to his captive's nose with his free hand.

"Vapron," he said, speaking for the first time, his voice deep and quiet.

"I don't need it, stud."

Most of the comrades used Vapron as a sex stimulant, but Dort seldom bothered. He knew from experience that the State-approved drug worked slowly, increasing the fly-free sensations; but when the cartridge stayed in place, he sniffed the sweet-sharp scent, then inhaled deeply once, twice.

The man gripped Dort's arm, steering him into the blackness. There were muffled voices and the sounds of male sex, and the stranger guided Dort as if he could see in the dark.

They went into a grass-floored room with night glow filtering through the broken roof overhead, just enough light for Dort to see that the man was peeling off his clothing. Following suit, he stripped, and the first tingling effects of the Vapron brought his dick stiff-up again. Then he was locked to the stranger, both of them naked and aroused. He felt the stud's ram, more than a match for his own.

The two comrades sank to their knees, clamped together in the traditional opening of sex combat. Then Dort was pressed down on his back, the burly stranger beside him. Strong fingers roamed over his chest, smoothing the slick hair and testing the coned nipples. Dort closed his eyes, slipping further into the drug-induced world of sensual excitement. The hands wandered lower over his torso, and Dort groaned with pleasure as the man gripped and stroked his rigid prick, then toyed with his pulsing testicles.

Now it was Dort's turn. He examined the stranger's stretched-out body as his had been examined, slowly, lazily. His fingertips traced the muscled flesh, slipping downward until he found the heat-swollen cock. He massaged it, fascinated at its powerful size and the crinkle-sacked balls beneath it.

Time ceased to exist. The two men writhed together with increasing desire. At last Dort was sprawled flat on top of his companion, and he buried his face in the crisp thicket of chest hair, inhaling the warm scent of masculinity, nuzzling each wide tit, lapping the sweat-damp silk in the broad armpits, tongue-washing the naked male, crouching to spit-lather the bulging cockhead, tasting, sucking, taking the massive shaft into his throat—if he weren't

5 x Clay Caldwell

Vapronized he might have choked and gagged—all the way down to the pubic wire at the base.

Dort felt the man twist and turn. A warm, wet mouth engulfed his throbbing hard-on. They suctioned each other rhythmically. Suddenly Dort was freed and hauled into the stranger's embrace. The capsule was held beneath his nose once more, and he inhaled without hesitation. This time the drug struck instantly, and he was catapulted into a fiery explosion of total release.

Vapron-free, Dort seemed to drift in a world of male sexuality, and he clung to the rugged stranger, moaning his pleasure. He was a First Level Trainee again, tromping around the dormitory bareass and matching his body with the other boys playfully. He was at Second Level, hung big and getting his cock sucked, sucking, fucking, getting fucked, enjoying all the State-provided satisfactions.

In the darkness of Impact Park's ruins, the taste of the man's cock lingered in Dort's mouth, and his nuts ached with sex-fire the way they had when he had been a horny, always-ready-for-anything Trainee. He let himself be turned over and laid out facedown, and he floated back to a forgotten time, one of the drug-induced effects. Fingertips crawled over his back and butt, and he was in the Third Level again, sprawled on the cleansing-room floor, one of his comrades eager to fuck his ass for the first time. He tried to remember that youth's name but couldn't. And then the stranger was kneeling between his spread legs, stroking his upturned buns.

Dort knew he was going to get rammed by the man's massive prick, but he didn't resist. Shit, he usually took the top role, humping the hell out of a willing stud. Then a muscled arm slid beneath his hips, raising him on his knees. The well-greased cockhead nudged into the cleft between his asscheeks and centered on the puckered opening, and he knew he'd never taken as big a male iron.

Arrrrrgggghhhhh!

He choked back a cry of pain as the swollen column drove flange-deep into him, and he dug his fingers into the soft dirt. The man held still, letting the flesh ring adjust to the initial penetration. Then he hauled Dort back to sit upright on the rigid prod. The hardness filled Dort's guts as the strong hands pawed over his chest and torso. He spun in the Vaproned world, accepting the potent invader, and he let his head slump back against the man's shoulder.

"Dort," the stranger whispered. "We fit, mate."

"Awww, yeah!" Dort moaned, submitting to the overwhelming sex combat. "Goddamn cock feels so good! Fuck me, stud! Slow and hard! Yeahhh!"

The thrusts began, lazy piston strokes, then sharp jabs. Dort pitched forward on all fours, and workrough palms raked his nakedness. Hoarse, excited breathing echoed in his ears, and flaming colors lit his clenched eyelids. Fingers enclosed his turgid dick and churning testicles, and the pain merged with pleasure. He howled as his climax surged free in ropy bursts of cum. The male column was quivering deep inside him, the man pinning him to the cool grass.

"Mate!" Dort wasn't sure if it was his voice or the stranger's. "Mate!"

The final stage of Vapronization was a slow descent, the two men joined together, the huge ram softening in

5 x Clay Caldwell

Dort's ass, the lips and tongue washing his sweaty shoulders, the complete union...the slow withdrawal...the weariness...the emptiness.

Unknown time later, Dort struggled to his feet. He wasn't surprised that the stranger was gone—that's the way it happened with Vapron sex combat. He found his clothes and dressed, still relishing the aftershocks of the experience.

By the time he had worked his way through the ruins of Impact Park and back to the open street, he was recovering. Then he spotted the two Forcemen beside the autotransit at the curb.

He'd always been intrigued by the State orderkeepers, and these two were typical, both good-looking, one blond, the other a redhead, each wearing a body-tailored uniform, each with a rapstick attached to his belt as a symbol of authority.

Dort wondered how Forcemen were selected, and by whom.

"Friend," the blond said to Dort, using the usual Forceman greeting. "I'm Blok." He nodded to the redhead beside him. "This is Ril." He showed an easygoing smile. "Identity?"

"I'm Dort." He reached for his card, and his back pocket was empty. "Shit, I must've dropped it in the park."

"Lost identity?" Ril asked. "We'll have to take you to Protection."

For an instant, Dort wanted to run, to escape. Then he saw Ril raise his nightstick. Dort had been trained to obey Forcemen, and he knew the crippling spark the stick could deliver. Numb, he got into the rear compartment of the transit, saw the uniformed men settle in front, heard the door latches click, felt the autodrive hum as they were set on the traffic pattern to Protection.

Dort had been to Protection before. Every youth was taken to the windowless headquarters of the Forcemen as part of his training, and he tried not to remember his last visit. No, Blok and Ril were his State-appointed friends, and they'd take care of the lost identity card. Sure.

The transit eased to a landing, and Dort was escorted into a brightly lit corridor, Blok on one side, Ril on the other. They passed a handsome Forceman followed meekly by a head-down, naked Zedro, and Dort couldn't help admiring the slave's muscular, shaven body. Forcemen had the best of everything, including Zedros.

They entered an unfurnished room with a hygiene alcove at one side.

"Strip, Dort," Blok ordered quietly. "Use the cleansing unit."

Automatically, Dort peeled off his clothing and went into the alcove to position himself behind the plastishield. The cycles began, and he could see the two Forcemen gathering up his clothes and examining them for contraband, then viewing his nakedness through the shield. The sprays drove into his cheeks-spread ass and spanked his genitals, and he felt his dick puff up as he remembered that sex combat with the stranger in Impact Park. Hell, it had happened only an interval ago, and here he was, horny as always!

Machine-washed and -dried, he returned to the other room. The Forcemen took him farther down the corridor and into a narrow office. A burly black-haired

Officer sat behind a large desk, his strong features highlighted by steady eyes, thin lips, and a cleft chin. The shirt of his uniform was wallpapered to his massive shoulders and barrel chest, a tuft of dark silk showing at the open collar.

"Shit!" Dort sank into the chair, unafraid. "I must've dropped it in Impact Park. You can check the computabs in my clothes."

"Maybe you stole the outfit." He gazed at Dort intently. "What were you doing in the park?"

"The usual. Sex combat."

"Any good?"

"Damn good," Dort admitted, then shrugged. "I was loaded on Vapron."

"Compumated?" Torg asked, suddenly changing the subject. "If you were, you'd have an alibi, and you wouldn't need to hunt the park."

"I'm not the one-stud type. I like to hunt."

Torg swung to his feet, his powerful physique clearly outlined beneath his uniform. He moved around to sit on the edge of the desk facing Dort, viewing his nakedness.

"How come you aren't a Forceman, Dort? You're good-looking, built, hung."

"I applied after Youth Training. No response." He felt an odd attraction to the man, and he stared at the male-bulging crotch of Torg's trousers, then dared to make the kind of remark he had used often at Impact Park. "Hey, stud, want to match meat?"

Torg's expression froze. He then nodded to the two Forcemen standing behind Dort. A moment later, Dort felt the blunt tip of a rapstick touch between his shoulder blades. An electroshock spilled him from the chair to his hands and knees on the concrete floor. The two men stood over him, tapping him again and again as if knowing each supersensitive point of his body, and finally a stick slid between his spread thighs and touched his testicles. He howled in agony and sprawled flat, clawed at the flooring, wanting to pass out. No, he wasn't allowed to escape into unconsciousness.

Torg signaled an end to the torture. Ril and Blok hauled Dort back onto the chair. He slumped forward, clutching his aching balls, as fingers gripped his hair and jerked his head up.

"From now on you answer questions, not ask them," Torg instructed gently. "You're going to spend a lot of time talking to me."

"Damn it," Dort mumbled, looking up at the man towering over him, "I haven't done anything illegal."

"Everything about you is imprinted on your card." He held a plasticard in one hand and casually splintered it. "We'll have to reestablish your identity, step by step." Dropping the shreds, he ran his fingers over the side of Dort's face almost affectionately. "Remember your first jerk-off match?"

"Hell, no. It must've been in Training."

"Your first blowjob? The first time you sucked? Fucked? Got fucked?"

"I—I don't remember."

"You will."

Torg pulled back, motioning to Blok and Ril. The two Forcemen dragged Dort to his feet and took him to another windowless room, unfurnished except for a waist-high, body-shaped table, a metal bar at the far end.

"Ever been in the saddle before?" Blok asked.
"Yeah. When I screwed up in Second Level."
"Assume the position, friend."

Taking a deep breath, Dort placed his feet in the metal half-shoes set well apart at the base of the table, then stretched forward, gripping the bar. His naked back and ass were presented to the Forcemen, and he glimpsed them peeling off their shirts, each exposing a solidly muscled torso. They slid the wide leather belts from their trousers and moved out of sight behind him. He squeezed his eyes shut and clenched his jaws.

Whack!

A hiss of pain whistled between his teeth as the lash ripped across his butt, and fiery lights seared the insides of his eyelids. He didn't try to escape because that would be a sign of weakness, and he had been trained to accept the authority of the Forcemen.

Whack!

The second blow fell from the other side, and Dort realized that Ril and Blok were taking turns lashing his bared flesh.

Whack!

Each carefully timed stroke was allowed to sink in before the next one was applied, and Dort remembered when he had been a Second-Level Trainee. He had been brought to Protection, stripped, and introduced to the saddle. He had tried not to cry out when the whips raked his ass. Okay, so he had ended up whimpering and promising never to break a Great State rule again. Later, when he was returned to the Training Center, all the youths in the dormitory knew from the glowing welts that he'd been disciplined.

Whack!

QSFx2

Dort wondered what might have happened to his comrades since those Training years. Maybe they had been compumated. Maybe they were getting their rocks off in the night shadows of a park. Maybe...

Whack!

A hoarse groan broke from Dort's throat. He hated the sound. He had been trained to be a strong member of the Great State, and...

Whack!
Whack!

He moaned. *Whack!* His pained howl echoed in his ears. *Whack!* He struggled. His body betrayed him. *Whack!* He was screaming. *Whack!* He was beaten. *Whack!!!*

Half-conscious, Dort realized that the whipping had ended. He felt the two men supporting him, helping him stumble down another corridor. Their arms were strong; their half-stripped bodies were warm and sweat-damp against his.

He was in a narrow cell, no windows, a dull light glowing overhead, a pad on the floor, a hygiene alcove beyond.

"When the light goes out, you sleep," Blok said as if repeating a speech he had given before. "When the light comes on, you get up and take your nourishment pills. Use the cleansing unit and shaving mask to prepare yourself. Maybe you'll be with Torg again, maybe with Ril and me."

The door clanked shut behind Dort, and he spilled onto the pad. He tried to sort out what had happened: the ordinary walk to Impact Park, the stud who had picked him out in the darkness of the ruins, the Vapron capsule held under his nose, the match of naked bodies, the animallike hunger, the mouth on his rigid cock and the male ram pulsing in his throat, more Vapron, then the potent iron fucking his ass—the total oneness!—and the Forcemen outside the park as if waiting for him, as if waiting to bring him to Torg.

The light snapped off, and Dort drifted asleep in spite of the pain of his beaten ass, a deep, dreamless rest as if he were Vapronized again.

The lights blinked on. Dort responded to the orders he had been given: getting up, taking the nourishment pills, then using the cleansing unit and shaving mask. He had barely finished when the cell door opened and Ril sauntered in.

"Torg's waiting."

Dort followed the bare-chested redhead down the hallway. He knew that anyone passing could see his welted butt, the sign of his disobedience to Great State.

He was led to Torg's office. The burly Officer motioned him to the straight-backed chair.

"We've searched the ruins at Impact Park, Dort. Your identity card wasn't found, so we'll have to reconstruct." He gave a slight smile, friend-like. "First memories?"

All of Dort's life was lasered into that lost chunk of plastic, and he was prodded into recalling his past by Torg's quiet questioning.

Sure, like all the comrades, he'd gone from Repro Center to Pre-Training, running nude with the other boys and laughing and giggling and falling asleep with any one of them. Then First Level, where they had been taught reading and writing and all. They had to wear Trainee uniforms in public, only to peel them off as soon as they returned to the dormitory. Yeah, Great State had taught Dort that the male body was nothing to be shy about, and he couldn't wait to get stripped.

"First full-cum?"

"Hey, I'd forgotten about that," Dort replied with a snicker. "Shit, that goddamn Log!"

Dort was in Second Level, joking around and tugging the other guys by the balls, growing bigger all over. One night they jumped on him and held him down on his pad. "First cum!" Log yelled and gripped Dort's thickened cock, pumping it to full hardness. Trapped, Dort felt his closest comrade fist his prick until that thick juice sprayed out. It felt so good that he laughed and clung to Log and drifted to sleep glued to him.

The questioning continued, and Dort found himself throwing a hard-on as he recalled his youthful experiences. Torg seemed almost pleased, and Dort wondered what the rugged Officer would look like naked with his stiffened prick jutting from his groin.

At last Dort was taken back to his cell. The light went off, he fell on his pad, and when the light came on again, he went through the ritual of nourishment pills, cleansing and shaving, finally waiting.

Ril and Blok came in, neither wearing shirts, and they took him down a hall to a room where his wrists were locked together with skintight plastitape. It seemed strange that they would bind him, but then he heard the whirr of a motor as a heavy chain lowered from the ceiling. Blok attached it to Dort's cuffed hands while Ril spread his legs and placed his ankles in floor clamps. The motor sounded again, and he was drawn upward, stretched, held securely.

"When was the last time you had sex combat?" Blok asked, running his fingertips over Dort's strained torso.

"Impact Park," he answered, his gaze fixed on the golden peach fuzz spun across the Forceman's chest. "Before you and Ril brought me here."

"How long ago was that?"

"I don't know." He shook his head as if trying to clear invisible cobwebs. "The light in my cell goes on and off, like there's no real time."

"You must need plenty of combat," Ril said, and he moved in to apply a cuplike device to Dort's testicles. "This'll set you up."

The two men left, and Dort felt a gentle tingling envelop his balls—not painful, but exciting. He thought about the times he had had a stud lick and suck his nuts until he was blast-hot, and he wondered how long it had been since that night in the park when he had shot his load while the stranger fucked his ass. The sensations mounted, and he dropped his head to see his cock throb and stiffen. He ached for the relief of climax, but just as he reached the moment of explosion, the torment stopped. Damn it, he needed to get his rocks off!

Ril returned and removed the cup from Dort's testicles, ignoring his swollen prick. A few minutes later, Blok returned, followed by a naked male with the hair on his head trimmed to the skullcap of a Zedro. His shaved body emphasized the play of his muscles, the untanned strip at his hips accenting the mature fullness of his genitals. His hands clasped behind his back in the State-prescribed manner, the Zedro knelt before Dort and nuzzled his pumped-up nuts as the two Forcemen shifted beyond his line of sight.

"Suck!" he hissed. "Suck my meat, Zedro!"

The kneeling man took Dort's iron into his mouth, swallowing it all the way to the wire-matted base. Without warning, a braided lash seared across Dort's shoulders. He gave a sharp cry. A second whip raked his butt as the Zedro began sucking.

Caught between the fiery pain of the strokes on his back and the taunting suction on his dick, Dort thrashed in his bindings. In spite of the brutal beating, his prick stayed erect and pulsing, and the Zedro continued to nurse it with expert skill.

Dort sank into a swirling sea of numbness. He heard his own agonized whimper vaguely each time the lash ripped his bare flesh, but it seemed as if he were off somewhere else, separated from his whipped body. At the same time, he was keenly aware of the mouth suctioning his inflamed ram, and he finally felt the churning fury of climax rise in his loins. He threw his head back and bellowed as the pleasure-pain consumed him, and the first burst of his cum tore free—then more, more, more!

Drained and exhausted, Dort realized the whipping had ended, and he moaned as his supersensitive dick was licked clean and released.

The Forcemen took the Zedro out of sight, and Dort hung like a slab of beaten meat, maybe hearing the sounds of sex conflict, maybe a dream, maybe Ril and Blok using the shaven slave.

Finally the two men returned, their faces and chests glistening with sweat. When they freed Dort, his legs turned to rubber. They caught him before he could fall, one on each side, and they hooked his arms over their shoulders to support him as they dragged him into the corridor leading to his cell. He felt the warmth and strength of their half-stripped torsos against his nakedness, and he relaxed, strangely content.

They laid him belly down on the pad, and strong fingers covered his battered back and ass with the coolness of quick-heal ointment.

"This'll fix you up in a hurry," Blok said. "You'll be in shape for your next session."

The Forcemen left, and even before the light went out, Dort fell into a deep sleep.

Light on. Ritual of nourishment pills and hygiene. Sometimes another discipline session, sometimes more questioning from Torg. Light off. Again... again... again...

"When was the last time you used Vapron?"

Dort was in the straight-backed chair before Torg's desk and he felt that odd attraction of being with the burly Officer. Yeah, Torg had been in charge of the beatings and tortures Dort had suffered, but there was something about him...

"That stud in Impact Park," Dort answered. "Maybe he thought I needed it for sex combat."

"And the first time?"

"Just before I graduated from Third-Level Training."

"It's illegal for Trainees to use Vapron."

"Log got a capsule somehow." Dort knew he was going to dredge up another almost-forgotten memory and spill it to the rugged Officer. "He and I and Kir sneaked down to the group-hygiene room after lights out so nobody would know what we were doing."

QSFx2

The three naked youths crept into the darkness. Log opened the capsule hung by a thong around his neck, inhaling deeply, then passing it to Dort. Dort sniffed warily, then took a full breath the way Log had. He didn't feel any change.

"Nothing," he grumbled.

"The stud who gave it to me said it takes time," Log whispered, offering the Vapron to Kir. "And keep it quiet, huh?"

Dort felt fingers stroke his heavy genitals, and the sex heat rose slowly, lazily. A hand rose over his sparsely haired chest, and he found himself examining his comrades. Sure, he'd had combat with both of them, and he knew Log's silk-thatched physique and thick cock as well as he knew Kir's sleek body and arrow-tipped prick.

They sank to the cool floor and crawled over each other, touching and licking, dicks swelling. Dort fell willingly into a world of thrashing masculinity. His lips found inflamed cocks and tight-sacked balls, and he tongue-washed muscled flesh and heated nipples. At the same time, hungry mouths and hands were moving over his nakedness, and he inhaled the heady scent of sweat-damp bodies.

Log passed the Vapron capsule again. This time the effect was immediate. Dort felt his heart pound in his chest, and he saw flaring colors swirl on the insides of his closed eyelids. Then he plunged into the totality of sex combat, gulping on Log's iron and nuts, shifting to Kir, lying back while lips and tongues explored every part of his body...endless time...trading places... giving ...taking...more...more!

Somewhere in the fiery haze, Kir was sprawled on his back, and Dort hunched over him, face to crotch, trading blowjobs. He shoved his hard-on downward into Kir's mouth and throat while he sucked the youth's rigid iron, then felt Log crouch behind him, strong hands pressing his buttcheeks apart, lubed fingers searching out his virgin asshole. Sure, Dort had rear-ended lots of Trainees, but he'd never been fucked before. On the other hand, Log was his closest comrade, and they were all floating on Vapron.

Log's solid cockhead centered on the tender opening, pressured. There was a flash of pain as it drove inward. If Dort cried out, the sound was muffled by the hard-on he held throat-deep. Then his muscle-ring seemed to relax. The man-shaft slid into him, filling his guts and pumping. He suctioned Kir's rod and drove his ram into the youth's mouth in rhythm with the potent penetrations.

The three youths worked together as if in a dreamworld of total sexuality, timeless, ending only when Kir tensed and began spurting his load. Dort swallowed the steamy fluid, and then he was zooming into a steamy climax like none he had ever known before. He spun through flashing lights and shadows, his cum gushing into Kir's sucking mouth. He was vaguely aware of Log's final thrusts and breathy hiss as his comrade's iron convulsed in his asshole.

Exhausted, they hung together, drifting through the comedown that follows Vapronized sex combat, until finally they slipped apart and moved to share the hygiene unit. They revived under the multiple sprays and, after the drying cycle, Kir snickered and groped Log and Dort playfully, then dashed toward the main room of the dormitory.

Without a word, Log went to the wall dispenser and

filled his palm with lubricant. He applied it to Dort's limp rod. Dort realized that Log was willing to get fucked but wasn't sure he could get another hard-on so soon after that last blast, so he and Log shared the Vapron capsule again. Instantly, Dort was on fire and cock-stiff. Then Log was on his hands and knees, asscheeks spread and offered.

Dort knelt behind his comrade and snaked his ram into the puckered opening as his brain exploded in searing light and frightening blackness. He seemed to feel unseen hands examining him. A huge naked man appeared in front of Log, forcing his massive iron into the youth's mouth. Another nude male straddled Log facing Dort, and a fiery prick drove into his throat. A hand reached forward between his thighs and gripped his throbbing testicles. A finger wormed into his asshole, then more, then a broad-knuckled hand. His pain-filled screams were muffled by the powerful flesh-column he was sucking; and unable to escape the fist clenching his balls and the one probing his guts, he was overwhelmed by the combination of agony and pleasure.

Dort hammered his iron into Log brutally, in endless thrusts, and finally thick, potent cum poured into his mouth. He drank it down as his own climax tore through him. Each shot was separate and distinct, gushing in racking waves, again and again until he was drained. Then the nightmare was over and he was clamped against Log's back, licking his fevered flesh and sinking into the post-Vapron haze.

When Dort returned to reality, he was alone. He dragged himself to the hygiene unit. Once more, the Great State machine cleansed him, and he stumbled to his pad in his cell, sprawled flat, and tumbled into a deep, dreamless sleep.

"You overdosed," Torg said when Dort had finished his memory. "Is that why you don't use Vapron often?"

"Hell, I don't need that stuff when I'm turned on to a stud." He looked down at his glistening hard-on, then grinned at the burly Officer. "I wonder why I get turned on when you and I—"

"Maybe you and Log were compumated," Torg interrupted.

"Shit, I don't want to be tied down to a mate—you know that. Anyway, he disappeared." Dort dropped his head, frowning. "Kir said he was brought here to Protection. But Kir was full of crap like that."

"Impact Park," Torg changed the subject with his usual abruptness. "You got your ass fucked, right?"

"I already told you about that. I was on Vapron."

"But you don't need Vapron." He nodded to the two Forcemen Dort hadn't noticed come into the office. "Take him."

Blok and Ril, bare chested, seized Dort and led him to the room where the saddle stood waiting. As before, he fitted his feet into the floor pads and stretched forward over the table to grip the metal bar at the far end, but this time his wrists were plastitaped to the rod and a mask was placed over his face, cutting out light and sound.

Helpless, he expected a bonecrushing beating, but instead fingertips scraped over his upturned ass and spread his buns. A greased, sharp-tipped cockhead centered on his exposed asshole, and he moaned through clenched teeth as it rammed into him. He knew it must be one of the Forcemen—Blok or Ril—

and his body relaxed, accepting the violent thrusts. Within the blackness of the mask, he relived the last time he had been fucked, Vapronized by the rugged stranger in the darkness of Impact Park.

When the first Forceman was satisfied, the second one took his place. Maybe there were more after that.

Dort's world was confused. When the light went on in his cell, he responded automatically, eating the nourishment pills, using the hygiene unit and shaving mask, being taken to be tortured or to be questioned by Torg, maybe going down on the two Forcemen who had fucked his ass, maybe plowing his ram into a Zedro bent over the saddle, maybe...

"I'm all mixed up," Dort confessed to Torg. "I'm not sure what's real and what isn't. How long I've been here. Why. The Zedro who sucked me, or did I do that to him? Ril and Blok?" He shook his head in bewilderment. "Awww, Torg! Help me work it out!"

"Sure." He touched Dort with that almost-affectionate stroke he'd used so often before. "How?"

"Let me see your cock," Dort's gaze fixed on the Officer's heavy mounded crotch. "I want to hold it, to taste it, suck it, take it up my ass, anything you want."

"Why?"

"It would be real, not a dream."

"Maybe, maybe not." Torg paused, then drew a deep breath and nodded to a uniformed Forceman Dort had never seen before. "He's ready."

Dort had grown accustomed to having Blok and Ril torture and use him. He felt uneasy with this stranger as he was taken into another room, empty except for a hygiene unit. He had used the unit in his cell before the interrogation session with Torg, but he obeyed the order to enter. The plastishield was closed, and he waited for the cleansing cycle to begin. Instead, he felt a tingling at the top of his head, like the shaving mask, and he saw his hair swirl about him and descend to the outlets at his feet.

Head down, Dort wondered if he was having another of those crazy dreams as he watched the electronic beams peel the fleece from his arms and chest and move steadily lower. The thicket of pubic wire at his groin disappeared, and his cock stiffened as the tingling sensations crawled over his testicles and into the slit between his asscheeks. Then his legs were stripped, and he felt more naked than ever before when he was brought from the unit.

The Forceman covered Dort's head with a mask, and he almost panicked until Vapron-tinged air pumped into his nostrils. Unable to see or hear, he was guided to another place and lifted easily onto a table. His arms and upper torso were bound in place by heavy straps. Cuffs were attached to his ankles, and his legs were raised at right angles to his body.

"This is the first time you've seen Revok Training, Blok?" Torg asked the handsome blond slouched in the chair next to him.

"Right." Blok moistened his lips. "What goes?"

"Dort's nourishment pills have been dosed, so he's dissociated. He doesn't know time or place, reality or dreams." He studied Dort's reaction as the Forceman eased a narrow plastipipe into the helpless captive's exposed asshole. "Revok is computerized. Once the equipment is in place, the machine takes over, judging Dort's reactions and endurance."

"He's tough," Blok murmured. "The pipe?"

"It feeds warm liquid into his guts until his belly swells up like it's about to bust. Then it drains and starts again. Now he gets the balls cup."

"Ril and I used one on him. He blasted like crazy."

"This time it'll keep working him up until he's empty." Torg watched intently as the Forceman completed the preparations. "The suction pump on his cock feels like a combination of a hot mouth and a supertight butthole, and the tabs on his tits stimulate them, tongue-licks at first, painful later."

"Goddamn!" Rick muttered. "He's already throwing a hard-on!"

"He's a horny stud," Torg said with undisguised pride as the machine bleeped and started. "Inside the mask, he's hearing the recordings we made of his discipline sessions and sex combat. He'll pop fast the first time."

Dort's prick swelled, filling the transparent tube. Suddenly it gushed thick cum.

"Man!" Blok exclaimed. "He sure shoots a load!"

"Before he goes soft, the sequence will begin again. When he's drained, Revok forces him to a final, impossible climax." Torg got to his feet and crossed to the table, viewing Dort's nakedness. "The asspipe expands and pumps like a fucking iron. The cup tightens and throbs on his nuts. The suction hammers his cock, and the titclamps bite. A prick-size gag jams into his mouth, overdosing him with Vapron. And then he blanks and becomes a Zedro."

"How come, Torg?"

"We're compumatched—I checked that before I had combat with him at Impact Park. But he doesn't believe in mating. As a Zedro, he won't have any choice." He ran his fingers over Dort's sweaty torso. "He'll go through intervals of rest and instruction, over and over, days and weeks, and he'll end up a Zedro."

"You're hot for him?"

"As hot as you and Ril are for each other." He spun toward the blond. "Until Dort's trained, you and Ril are going to take me off. Understand?"

"Yes, sir." Grinning, Blok dropped to his knees in front of the Officer. "Give me that ram of yours, friend!"

Dort woke up when the overhead light in his cell snapped on, and he downed his nourishment pills automatically and went into the hygiene alcove. As if programmed, he used the cleansing unit. He frowned in confusion when he applied the shaving mask and studied his reflection in the mirror. The hair on his head was close-cropped in a bristle cap, but lower. Glistening silk was sprayed across his high-arched chest. A Zedro should be body-shaved, and he was reassured of his status when he stepped back and saw the telltale strip of untanned flesh at his hips, his heavy prick dangling from a forest of pubic wire.

"Zedro," he whispered proudly. "Zedro!"

He returned to the other room and took the prescribed position, head down, hands locked behind his back.

After uncounted time, the door opened.

"I'm Torg," a strong masculine voice said. "What's your name?"

"A Zedro doesn't have a name, sir."

"I'll call you 'Dort.' You've been assigned as my personal Zedro."

"Yes, sir."

"You'll be living with me. C'mon."

Obediently, Dort followed the man from the cell. It didn't make any difference where they were going or what he might be required to do. He was a Zedro, conditioned to serve, to be used, whipped, beaten, tortured—whatever his Master demanded. Even so, he felt a strange attraction to the Officer called Torg, a willingness to be his slave.

They walked through a maze of hallways, passing uniformed Forcemen and naked Zedros. Then Torg was inserting an identity card into a door slot. Dort didn't have a card because he was a Zedro.

Torg led the way into a living cubit, and Dort assumed the proper stance, eyes clamped shut as the Officer stripped off his clothing.

"Check out the place," Torg ordered. "I'm going to clean up."

Dort waited until Torg was in the hygiene unit before he scrambled to gather up the uniform and jam it into the cleaning chute. He paused to view the spacious room, the masculine furnishings dominated by an oversized sleeping pad. He had the peculiar feeling that he had been selected by Torg for a reason.

Troubled, he went to the large window at the end of the cubit and stared out at Great State City. He knew the dimming light was called sunset, to be followed by night and then day.

"That's Impact Park on the horizon," Torg said, coming up behind Dort. "Ever been there?"

"I don't know, sir."

"Turn around, Dort. Take a look at me."

"Yes, sir."

Dort faced the naked man and gazed at him with

open curiosity. Torg's short-clipped black hair framed his rugged features, and his thick neck was flanked by powerful shoulder muscles. The barreled curves of his chest were washed with dark silk, and his solid torso was deep bronze. Between his heavy thighs, his massive cock fell over his loose-slung testicles, and he fingered the vein-marked shaft with the hint of a grin.

"Ever seen me before, Dort?"

"I don't think so," Dort answered solemnly. "I'd remember a stud like you." He dropped his head, frightened at his brashness. "I shouldn't have said that, sir."

"Shit!" Torg exploded. "When we're alone, you can do anything you damn please."

"I want to touch you, sir."

"Go ahead."

Gingerly, Dort raised his hands to Torg's chest. He watched his fingers stroke the tangled hair and examine the wide, firm nipples. Then Torg embraced him, squirming against the masculine nakedness.

"Torg," he murmured. "Torg!" He took a fast breath. "Is it okay if I throw a hard-on, sir?"

"What if I say no?" Torg asked, pulling back and gripping Dort's swelling prick.

"I'd have to disobey you, sir."

"Goddamn!" the Officer roared, laughing. "Get over on the sleeping pad, Dort! It's time we had some all-out combat!"

Dort liked the sound of Torg's laughter, and he spilled onto the pad, pleased as he watched the cock-hot man approach. Torg settled on his side next to Dort and ran one palm over the Zedro's hard-plated chest.

"Torg? How come I'm not shaved like the other Zedros?"

"I wanted you the way you are." He stroked Dort's upturned torso with tantalizing slowness. "Ever been shaved?"

"I must have been." He hesitated. "I—I don't remember anything before you came to my cell today."

"You'll remember everything from now on."

"I sure hope so, sir." He gripped Torg's hand and carried it downward to his exposed genitals, then relaxed as his inflamed prick and crinkle-sacked testicles were fingered and inspected. "I'm your personal Zedro—that's what you said. You can do anything you want with me, but I'll go right on being your Zedro."

"Like we're compumated, huh?"

"Zedros can't compumate," Dort replied, and then he felt he had spoken out too sharply. He expected the hand holding his nuts to clench and take him into a withering agony. When it didn't happen, he wrestled Torg down on his back. "I want to service you, sir."

"Shit!" Torg chuckled, amused by the Zedro's determination. Dort fell on him, grinding their bodies together hungrily. "Go ahead, mate!"

Somehow Dort knew all the things that would arouse and please the Officer. He nuzzled the lush chest hair, nursed the heated nipples, lapped each broad, silk-filled armpit, worked lower and lower over the powerful physique. He felt an unexpected delight in the scent and taste of Torg's body, the sound of his excited breathing.

At last Dort was sprawled between Torg's legs, and he gazed for a moment at the potent genitals. Then he pressed Torg's massive iron back to expose his testicles, and he hunched forward to lick them. He sucked first one and then the other, finally taking both of them into his mouth together. Again, he seemed to know instinctively when he had suctioned long enough. He released the balls and ran his tongue tip up the taut undercord of Torg's cock. At the tip, he found the stickiness already drizzling over the bulging crown, and he was proud of having gotten the stud so horny. Eagerly, he gulped down the vein-etched shaft, wetting it and drawing it into his throat with ease.

Torg hissed with pleasure. Then he was twisting opposite Dort, sucking the Zedro's prick! It didn't seem right that a Forceman should be going down on a Zedro, but Dort told himself that the Officer could do anything he wanted with him. He closed his eyes. He felt as if he might have done this before, sometime, somewhere, in the darkness...Torg!

Maybe sensing that Dort was about to cream, Torg wrenched free.

"Lie back, Dort. I'm going to screw your ass." He reached to the wall dispenser beside the pad and filled his palm with lubricant. "Vapron?"

"Not allowed, sir." He watched the burly man grease his hard-on and move into position, face-to-face. "Anyway, I'm your Zedro and—"

"Crap!" Torg raised Dort's legs and massaged his exposed asshole with glazed fingers. "Relax, mate!"

Dort tried to obey, but when the bulging cockhead centered and thrust inward, he choked back a scream of pain. For a long moment, neither man moved, allowing Dort's body to accept the initial penetration.

"Torg...yeah!!"

Torg inserted his rigid iron gently. When it was fully buried, he released Dort's legs and hunched forward over him, sweat-glowing.

QSFx2

"Do you like to fuck, Dort?"

"I think so. Why?"

"There's another Zedro here at Protection. He's named Log. He'll dig getting your ram up his butt."

"Could I work on your meat at the same time, Torg?"

"Hell, you're going to get it every way there is." He dropped forward on Dort, embracing him and beginning to hip-pump. "We fit real good, mate."

"Great State must have known that when I was assigned to you." Happy that Torg was calling him "mate," Dort locked his arms and legs about the surging man. "I belong to you, Torg."

"Damn right, mate!"

A Dort Called Tiger

I'm a Dort and damn proud of it.

The Nation channels most boys into Dort training almost as soon as we're hatched, but only a few of us graduate. I got a charge out of all those years of schooling, only it was hard when one of the guys I'd messed with was rechanneled. Shit, we all went bareass and slept clutched up to each other long before our peckers started acting man-grown.

It was my classmate Rak who nicknamed me Tiger after an extinct animal we learned about in ancient-history class. Ever heard of a tiger? It was a creature that leaped on others—something like I did, I guess.

So now I'm in the cleansing room, Rak and me readying ourselves for Dort duty. The warm sprays wash from all around, scraping us spotless inside and out. I remember my school days, the physical development sessions, the injections to pump up our muscles, the taste of Gron to relax me before the treatments to build my cock and balls, the first time I shot a load into the suction tube, all those growing-up times. Maybe Rak's remembering the same things because he's smiling at me and tugging his dick.

That goddamn Rak! He's built and hung a lot like me, but he keeps himself shaved from the neck down. Yeah, he'd have hair on his chest and around his prick and all, but he's baby-smooth all over. It sure shows off his muscles, and he's one of the most popular Dorts in the station. Hell, shacking up with that slick body gets me turned on, even if we're not allowed to have sex. We sleep together—that's all. I wonder what it would be like to be shaved like Rak, but the Chief Adviser said no when I asked permission.

"We're running late," I remind Rak as we stretch and turn in the drying cycle of our washdown. "We spent too much time in Physical Upkeep."

"You want to keep built, don't you?"

He knows the next step, and he grabs a cloth to wrap about his hips before I snap the Rays switch. The beams bronze me from head to toe, but Rak keeps his crotch and ass untanned. That's part of being a shaved Dort: showing those pale targets front and rear.

We head for the dressing room, stopping off for a cup of Gron, and the liquid hits my stomach with the usual warmth and relaxation. We slap at each other, just fooling around, and we pull on our cup-straps, buckling them in place. Right away the electronic tingle starts stirring my prick and balls, and I know Rak's getting as hard as I am. Crap, there's no way I can hold my rod down, but there's no room for it to grow, that's the reason for the cup. Between the Gron and the strap, I'm heating up fast.

"What's the duty tonight?" I ask Rak, pulling on my thigh-length jacket.

"A Guarian blast." Rak won't wear a jacket because he's shaved. "Brug'll be there. Maybe he'll finally hunk you."

"What makes you think so?"

"All he talked about was you when he hunked me."

"Bullshit," I say, taking the flash test to make sure I haven't picked up a pre-Nation disease like a cold in the nose or something else. "Brug's rough, huh?"

"Dorts don't blap about being hunked," Rak reminds me. "You know the rules."

"Yeah."

No Dort blaps about who's hunked him, not even a Guarian. Guarians are special-good, giving themselves to us Dorts, and I've had this strange urge to mess with the one called Brug. That's crazy because Dorts aren't supposed to feel anything special for a male stud.

Rak and I go into the game room, and the air is heavy with sex-scent and the throb of antisound. The Guarians wear knee-length robes tied with a belt at the waist while the other Dorts are dressed like me, except for Rak. We pick up flasks of Gron and move into the crowd, filling empty goblets. I feel a hand stroke up my thigh, and I look down at a Guarian already stripped, one I've grouped with at another time. Most Guarians dig group-hunkers, us Dorts swarming all over them, servicing them anyway they want, and my cock aches to be released from that lousy cup-strap.

I hear Rak's hoarse groan, maybe getting his strap torn off, maybe getting his shaved body played with, maybe servicing men front and rear. I go on doing my duty as a Dort.

Brug!

The black-haired Guarian stands alone in the shadows, a glimpse of dark chest silk showing at the top of his robe, harsh-cut features, narrowed eyes fixed on me. He's never joined in group-sessions so I've never seen him stripped, but I suspect he's got one hell of a body. He wets his thin lips and raises his goblet, indicating that he wants more Gron. I go to him simultaneously numb and aroused.

"I want you, Tiger," he says quietly. "I've held back long enough." He sips the Gron I've poured for him. "No group-action. Just you and me. Willing?"

"Yes, sir," I answer obediently, thinking it's odd that he's asked me if I'm willing. A Dort mustn't say no, especially to a Guarian. I have this crazy feeling that I couldn't say no to Brug, no matter what.

He nods and opens a door behind him, and I follow him down a hallway to a dim-lit room, a broad deck covered with thick padding at one side, a shelf lined with flasks of Gron and lubes and whips and who knows what other torture instruments. Brug closes the door and snaps the lock. There is sudden silence because the walls are soundproof. I have seen Dorts who have been used in this room. No, Rak didn't come back marked after his session with Brug, but maybe—

Brug faces me and holds the goblet to my lips. I drink thirstily. I'll need all the Gron I can get if this Guarian demands more than I have experienced. The heat rises through me, and the sex-urge takes over again.

"Now, Tiger," he murmurs.

He runs his hands over my jacket and spreads it open. He strokes my bared flesh. His fingers are work-rough but they graze lightly over my chest and nipples, then slide down my sides to the strap at my hips. He unfastens the buckles, and my swollen prick snaps free.

"Brug," I hear my voice choke. "Yeah, Brug!"

He opens his robe and locks me up against him. He's wearing a strap, and it grinds my naked cock and nuts. Thick silk covers his barreled chest, curling around his nipples and trailing downward over his slabbed abdomen, and he rubs my back and ass.

"You're a Dort," he reminds me. "Strip me."

I press the robe free from his massive shoulders and let it fall to the floor, and I run my fingers over his muscle-carved chest. I have never been with a man like this, not even other Guarians, and I sink to my knees and remove his cup-strap. Goddamn! His cock is longer and thicker than any I have serviced before, curling outward and down from a thick patch of pubic wire, almost hiding the loose-sacked testicles dangling behind it.

I want it!

I grip the shaft and bring the tip to my lips, kiss it, lick it, taste it, take it into my mouth, feel it swell with heat. He scrapes his fingers over my head, forcing me deeper onto his mounting iron, and he pulls back without warning. Maybe he'll punish me for not asking his permission. He grabs me under the arms and yanks me to my feet, and he lays me out on my back on the pad. He stands over me, a shadowed giant with his spit-wet prick spearing from his crotch, and he eases onto the pallet beside me.

"Tiger," he whispers, one hand roaming over my body. "Rak told me you're the best Dort in this station."

"Rak talks too much, but he never told me anything about you, especially not that you're horse-hung."

"You've got plenty of meat yourself." He marks my rigid hard-on, and I brace myself for the crippling pain when he grasps my churning balls. "I'm glad I worked through all those others before I got to you."

Goddamn Guarian! Sure, we've been sharing Gron, but it's more than that. I want him, not just to service him like all the others, and he's playing with me, close and gentle.

"Sonofabitch!" I bark and twist over to clamp against him. Okay, I'm breaking the rules by cursing and all, but I'll take my chances—I dunno why. "I'm going to drain you dry!"

"That's what Rak said," he chuckles, rolling over on his back. "That shaved Dort sure choked when he tried to gulp on my rod, and he cried out real loud when I entered his ass. Maybe you'll do the same when I do it to you."

"Bullshit!" I flip over on top of him, prick-to-prick, and I nuzzle his thick-corded neck. "I've been trained to make a stud like you beg for mercy!"

Damn right, I've been trained, and I'm going to show this bastard! I move down to his chest, lapping the soft hair washing the burly arcs, finding and sucking each firm nipple. His excited breathing echoes in my ears. Yeah, I'm getting to him, and I lick the sweaty silk in his armpits. He squirms beneath me, and I work lower, tonguing and washing and nibbling all the way to his crotch. Man, there's that giant cock standing straight up, vein-etched and glowing with heat, but I'm not ready to gulp on it yet. I go for his balls, hauling them down in their hair-spiked sac and licking them, and the lush scent of his groin is like another shot of Gron. I want to suck both of those rocks at once, but there's no Dort in the whole Nation with a mouth that can stretch enough for that so I'll settle for taking them one at a time.

Awww, they taste so good!

"Tiger!" he hisses. "Climb on my aching dick!"

I'm a Dort and I must obey. I press down on the base of the throbbing shaft and steer the crown to my lips. I wet it with my tongue and swallow the clear liquid bubbling from the piss slit. I want it, all of it! I stuff the monster into my mouth, and I will my throat muscles to relax and accept every inch of this male-ram.

Brug groans and rubs my shoulders. He locks his powerful legs about me, clamping me in place. He may break my ribs if I don't choke to death first! He releases me and hauls me up to rest beside him, and he raises my head to feed me another shot of Gron. Shit, I'm already asteroid-high from doing Dort-duty with him, and he's turning me on my side, my back to him. He spreads my asscheeks and lubes my hole. I know what he wants.

"Sir," I say respectfully, "I'm not sure I can take as much meat as you have."

"You're a Dort, Tiger."

"Yes, sir."

He centers his iron on my target and drives flange-deep. Too big! I stuff my fist in my mouth to smother my scream; I don't want him to know how much it hurts. He inches deeper, draws back, plugs again and again, giving me more of his hammer with each thrust, and I'm taking it. Yeah, I'll show this fucking Guarian how good a Dort I am.

"Open up, Tiger," he whispers. "I'm going all the way."

He clamps against me, and his ram slithers into my guts, filling me like never before.

"You're wrecking me," I groan. "You're ripping me apart!"

"Get used to it." He twists over on his back, carrying me with him, and he digs in his heels, raising his hips to impale me totally. "I'm going to hunk you every way there is. I'm going to turn you over so I can plow you face-to-face, so I can play with your tits and cock and balls, so I can see the look on your handsome face, so I can watch you take my load." His palms slide over my chest, and he chuckles. "I sweat hard when I hunk, so we'll shower together afterward. You'll lather me head to toe, Dort-style, and when we're spotless, we'll come back here and drink more Gron and talk. Then I'll hunk you plenty more." He grasps my flaming cock and rumbling balls. "When I'm done, you won't want any prick smaller than mine."

"I already feel that way, you sonofabitch."

"Maybe I'll apply to have you for a personal Dort."

Shit, I've never thought about servicing just one man. I'd have to leave the station, give up group showers, no more gang sessions, live with Brug, take his oversized iron whenever and however he wants—only him.

"I want you," I confess, secure in his embrace. "I'm going to make you forget every other Dort you've ever had."

"You already have." He raises my upper leg and turns me on my back easily, ram staying buried in my tail, and he looms over me on all fours, every muscle tensed, his eyes burning with sex-hunger. "Let's go, Tiger!"

"Yesssirrr!!"

Pro vs. Con

The river divides the Territory into two sections: one for the Pros, the other for the Cons. When a youth completes his coming-of-age education, he chooses which side of the river he will spend the rest of his life on. Pros and Cons respect each other's area and never mix; they stay on their side, we stay on ours. Yeah, I picked being a Pro.

This one night my balls were working overtime, so I cleaned up and pulled on a sport shirt which fit tight and pants that fit even tighter—the standard garb for a Pro on the prowl. I went down the street to the nearest social center, and after a couple of glasses of Terroise and a few uninteresting gropes, I decided to try another center.

I loafed outside, and I needed to take a leak so I stopped off at the nearest pissery. The single room was dark and evidently deserted, and I opened my fly and

QSFx2

let my pecker dangle while I unloaded the Terroise I'd stored up. Suddenly two figures came out of the shadows, one blond and tanned, the other black-haired and swarthy. Both wore leather jackets and trousers: the uniforms of Cons.

"What the hell are you bastards doing in Pro area," I barked.

"Hunting for a cocksucker like you," one of them answered.

"How about gulping on a man-sized chunk?" the other asked.

"A Pro go down on a Con?" I sneered. "That'll be the day!"

"I think we've got what we're after," the blond said, and he moved behind me, arm-locking my neck and wrenching my head back. "Dose him, pal."

The other man clamped a wet cloth over my face. When I gulped for air, a sweet scent paralyzed me, including my vocal cords. Helpless, I was hauled from the pissery. Anyone seeing us would think two buddies were taking an over-Terroised chum home. They dumped me in the back of an autovan and stretched out beside me, and the machine began moving on a precomputerized course. I was certain they were taking me across the river to the Con area, but I couldn't move or yell for help. No, I couldn't even defend myself when they opened my shirt and trousers and examined me.

"I'm Tray," the black-haired Con said, toying with my prick. "My comrade is Buzzer, and he sure picked a winner this time." He grinned, gripping my balls firmly, and the damp cloth covered my face again. "We're going to train you to beg for our meat, Pro."

I sank into swirling blackness. When I came to, I was stretched out naked on a table in a windowless room, the two leather-clad men looming over me.

"He's awake," Buzzer said, digging his fingernails into one of my nipples. "Welcome to your new home, Pro."

"Knock it off, you sonofabitch!" I bellowed.

"Make all the noise you want to," Tray snickered, twisting my other tit. "Nobody outside can hear, and I like hearing a Pro yell." He pulled back, smiling. "You're going to yell your guts out before we're done slaving you."

"I'll never be a slave! Especially to a couple of goddamn Cons!"

"Bullshit!"

They wrenched me from the table and slammed me face-forward against a wall. There was a soft hum as an electrofield pinned me in place. Yeah, these Cons had all the modes we Pros did.

Crack! The first belt slash across my ass made me gasp, but I clenched my teeth to keep from crying out as a second came from the other side. Slowly, making each stroke count, they whipped me from each side to keep the marks even, and I couldn't stop the groans, then the howls as the welts crisscrossed up and down my back. They continued the merciless beating until my throat was as raw from screaming as my backside was from being strapped; and when the electrofield was turned off, I crashed to my hands and knees. I got my brains cleared and looked up. Both men had taken off their jackets, showing powerful, thick-muscled physiques, except that Buzzer's barreled chest was dusted with golden peach fuzz while Tray's was blanketed with black silk. Hell, I would have mixed with either of them if they *weren't* Cons.

They jerked my head up and clamped a chain around my neck. I heard the buzz of a magnoweld as it was sealed in place. Then they took me to a small, unfurnished cell and dumped me on the floor, and I was left alone in total darkness. Naked, whipped, collar-chained, and aching, I tried to get into a comfortable position and rest. A calming voice surrounded me. "You are a slave," it told me. "You will serve your Masters."

The message was repeated endlessly, but somehow I was able to sleep, I don't know how long. Without warning Tray and Buzzer returned, and they fed me a dry, tasteless powder called Nutria which was to become my steady diet. Then they led me to a latrine and watched while I showered and shaved; later I realized they kept me clean-shaven so the stubble on my face wouldn't show the passage of time. Finally I was taken to the room where I'd been whipped and placed with my back against the electrofield wall, unable to move.

Buzzer started off by putting clamps on my nipples, and Tray followed by attaching a leather ballstretcher to my testicles. Each one took his time, Buzzer increasing the pressure on my tits, Tray adding weights to the stretcher. It seemed like hours before the combined pains rose to the point where I couldn't hold back my moans, and I screamed in agony when Tray tapped my strained testicles with his fingertips. Yeah, he liked hearing me howl, and he kept working on my nuts until I was barely conscious. That's when they freed me and draped me facedown across the table in the center of the room.

"You're going to beg to suck our cocks when we're finished training you," Tray declared, standing in front of me and pawing the mounded crotch of his trousers. "In the meantime, you'll take us off another way." He chuckled and nodded to Buzzer. "You're first, pal."

The next thing I knew, the burly blond was behind me, spreading my asscheeks and poking the lubed tip of his rod against my exposed hole. Hell, I'd been fucked before, but I cursed at the humiliation of being humped by a Con. Buzzer drove a huge cockhead into me, stretching me more than I'd thought possible, and he held collar-deep until my muscle-ring adjusted. Then he began inching his rigid shaft deeper and deeper, filling my guts almost gently and pumping slowly. No lie, it felt like he was screwing me with a macropole—that's how big he was hung. He took his time riding me. Finally he slammed down, blanketing me with his sweaty body and bellowing that he was shooting his load. Finished, he rested and softened. When he pulled out, I felt strangely empty—but only for a moment.

Tray took over, and he rammed inward in a single brutal plunge. His iron seemed as big as Buzzer's, but there was nothing gentle about the way he hammered me. I knew he wanted to hear me yell, and he got his wish. He pounded ruthlessly, and he gripped the chain around my neck to jerk my head back and give him more leverage. I couldn't breathe, and I passed out before he must have flooded my guts with more Con cream.

I came to in the darkness of my cell. The voice was chanting that I was a slave to my Masters.

After that, each session began with my ration of

Nutria, then a shower and shave and the walk to the room where I never knew what to expect. Maybe I'd be pinned against the electrofield wall and whipped until my ass was burned enough for them to fuck it. Maybe they'd zap me with a magnostick, sending stabbing shocks through whatever part of my body it touched—and they made sure it hit every part. One time they put me into a jockstrap with a cup that clamped my genitals tightly, and then they made me swallow a liquid they called KwikUp. In seconds a sex-rush hit me, making my cock heat up for the first time since I'd been made prisoner, but there was no way my rod could escape its bondage and grow full-hard. I know I begged to be allowed to jerk off, but they just laughed until the drug had worn off before screwing my tail.

Alone in my cell, I began to fantasize about how Tray and Buzzer looked without those leather pants. Sure, I had seen them bare chested and felt their rams crammed up my butt, but I'd never seen those tools totally exposed. I tried to picture them in the darkness, and all the time that voice was telling me that I was a slave. Maybe I was beginning to believe it.

The final session began, as always, with the usual feeding and washing; but when I was taken to the room, I was strapped faceup on the table. Small cups were placed on my nipples, my prick was inserted into a plastiform tube, and my balls were covered with a soft wrapping. A heavy dose of KwikUp was poured into my mouth, and when I swallowed, the sex-blast gave me a roaring hard-on. With a snicker, Tray flipped a switch, and I braced for jolting pain. Instead, the cups nibbled my tits, the tube suctioned my cock, and the wrapping licked my nuts. Believe me, it was the ultimate blowjob—even better than the gang action I'd experienced in Pro territory. Soon I was discharging the cream stored up since being kidnapped.

Look, when I'm warmed up, I'm good for two or three shots in a row—but the machine didn't give me time to rest and reload. It continued to pump my inflamed rod. I don't know how often I popped before what had been real pleasure became agony. Drained, my iron stayed hard, and I cursed, I howled, I begged for an end to this torture. My reward was another dose of KwikUp.

I floated in a warm world of exhaustion, and I heard the voice from my cell telling me that I was a slave and explaining how I was to serve my Masters. My numbed brain must have accepted the instructions because suddenly I was released from the bindings and equipment.

"Come here, slave," Tray ordered.

Automatically, I rolled off the table and crawled to him. I licked the legs of his pants and pressed my face against his full crotch to demonstrate my servitude. Buzzer stood beside Tray, and I repeated the rite on him. When I reached his crotch, Buzzer opened his fly, and for the first time I saw the tool that had plowed my ass so many times. It was long and thick. The glistening shaft was as smooth as polished ivory. He held it to my lips, and I took it into my mouth, licking and sucking, pleased with the masculine taste and scent of my Master. The column stiffened and slithered into my throat, and I rocked forward and back, gulping hungrily. I wanted to serve him. Without warning, he was firing blasts of rich, thick sperm. I drank every drop, and then Tray took over. Not only was he built like Buzzer, but he was hung as big, except that his hard-on was gnarled with swollen veins. He gripped my head and held me in place while he face-fucked me with the same fury he'd used on my tail. Soon I swallowed another load of cream.

My Masters no longer called me "Pro," merely "slave." I learned my duties quickly. Naked, I started my chores as soon as they left for their work assignments, and I was ordered to spend at least one hour using the exercise equipment in the sun-burning courtyard. My muscles hardened while I gained an all-over tan, and they seemed satisfied when they checked me out while I lathered them in the shower. They had separate bedrooms, but the three of us always slept together, me in the middle so I could suck one while the other plowed my butt. They gave me a leather uniform like theirs so I could go outside to run errands; only my jacket had a chain hung across it to show that I was a slave. Now that I was well trained, Tray took less interest in abusing me.

One Friday night, Buzzer called me into his room. He was lying back naked on the bed, the cool light gleaming on his blond hair and bronzed physique and heavy cock, and he ordered me to lie down beside him. He told me that Tray was out finding another Pro to train and that I would serve him alone for once. He swallowed a little KwikUp, then fed me a couple of drops. The reaction came slowly, gently, and my rod stiffened.

"I own you, slave," he said and ran his fingers over my chest and nipples. "I can do anything I want with you."

"Yes, sir."

His hand roamed lower and lower as if exploring me for the first time, and finally he toyed with my hard-on and churning balls.

"I can do anything I want with you," he repeated, and he shifted to kneel between my legs and take my prick into his mouth.

Shit, I hadn't had a blowjob since I'd been kidnapped, but this Con gulped on my horny meat like an expert. He sucked it head-to-nuts again and again, and I soared toward climax.

"Sir," I warned. "Master!...Buzzer!!"

I exploded in long, wrenching streams, and Buzzer swallowed all of it. Drained, my tool stayed erect, and he made me thrash and hiss as he licked it clean. Then he rested back, and I knew he needed to be served.

I played my fingers over his gold-fuzzed chest and worked downward until I reached his rigid cock. All I could think about was pleasing him, so I crawled over him, licking and sucking. When I finally lapped his bull-nuts the way he liked, he quivered and groaned.

"Suck, slave! Cool my aching prick!"

I took that slick column throat-deep as I'd learned to do, and in what seemed like seconds, I was gulping his boiling cream. He blasted in heavy spurts, and I swallowed it hungrily. Yeah, I wanted to truly satisfy my Master!

Finished at last, he hauled me up to him and locked me in a powerful embrace.

"You're the best slave a Con could ask for," he murmured, stroking my back and tail. "I'm going to fuck you front and rear all night long."

"Yes, sir!"

He wasn't fooling. We dozed a little. Then he brought us back to action with a few drops of KwikUp. He rode my butt, we showered and I sucked his iron, we slept together, and when I dared to call him "Buzzer," he chuckled and went down on me again, reminding me that I was his slave.

The next morning, I woke up alone. I hurried to perform my duties, certain that Buzzer and Tray were training another Pro. They wore their leather pants when they came for meals, but nothing was said about the Pro—not even when Buzzer and I climbed into bed at night. Then one day they ordered me into the room where I'd been trained, and there was this naked Pro on his knees, dark-haired like Tray, rugged-handsome, muscled, black silk swirled over his barreled chest, his back and ass lined with welt marks, his limp cock dangling over sagging eggs, a slave collar like mine permafixed around his neck. His glazed eyes said he'd been given the final treatment that had broken me.

"Suck him, Junior," Tray growled.

The new slave crawled forward to do a job on my iron. Later Buzzer told me they had named him "Junior" because he was lower in rank than me.

Junior shared the work with me, and I liked watching him pump his muscles on the exercise equipment. Afterward we would shower together, and I'd soap his dick to get him warmed up for Tray. He was hung as big as Tray with the same kind of vein-swollen shaft. Some nights Buzzer and I would hear the snap of a leather strap against bare flesh and Junior's groans. Yeah, Tray turned on to causing pain to his slave, and

Junior served him well. As a matter of fact, Junior seemed almost proud when he showed the black-and-blue marks.

"Ever think about escaping back to Pro territory?" Junior asked me one day when we were washing up after a workout.

"No." I was lathering his butt, and I slid a finger into the slit between his trim buns. "Right now I'm thinking about how good it'd be to fuck you." I pulled back reluctantly. "I'd better ask my Master's permission."

"You do whatever he says?" he asked, turning to nudge his hard-on against mine.

"I'm his slave," I explained, rubbing my palms over the water-soaked hair on his chest. "I belong to him, just like you belong to your Master."

"I swore I'd never be a slave when I was first brought here," Junior confessed, soaping my balls. "But now I feel damn special when my Master says I've done well serving his needs." Excited, he squeezed a little bit harder than I wished. "Think of all we would've left unknown about ourselves if we hadn't been trained!"

That seems to be the best way of explaining slavery.

Renegade

I've always been a loyal citizen of the Republic, and I obey all the rules. Without the rules, we wouldn't be safe and protected and free, right?

It's Friday afternoon, and when the chimes sound to mark the end of the work period, I make sure everything is shut down. I'm a crew leader, and a leader has to look out for his gang. I've got a damn good gang.

I loaf to the locker room, strip, and take my turn in front of the laser blast. That's another rule. Before and after each shit, we take a blast to detect contamination or disease. The Republic makes sure we aren't infected with one of those old-time bugs. In an instant I'm checked and cleared, and I head for the shower room.

Most of the guys are already here, joking and washing each other. Some of them are starting to show hard-ons, short or thick or long or whatever, just like always. There's no rule against messing around in the showers.

There's an empty space next to my buddy Hank, and when I take it, the spray whisks down at the Republic-set temperature. Hank's tall and lean muscled, and as soon as I'm wet, he reaches over to soap my cock and balls while I lather my chest and arms. We scrub each other the way we always do, and when he turns to have me wash his back, I work downward slowly, enjoying the feel of his slick flesh beneath my palms.

"We're going to jump Nick when he comes in," he says.

Nick's the newest member of our team, and he's going to be initiated with a session of gang-sex. I don't know if it's a rule, but every newcomer gets it.

"Hot for that little stud?" I slip a finger into the cleft in his tail and massage his puckered asshole. "Want to make it with him?"

"Shit," he mutters, but I know from experience that he digs getting rear-ended. "I'd like to have him blow me while you're dicking me."

"Yeah?" I pull away to finish my shower. "I'll let you know."

The rinse cycle begins, and Nick tromps into the room. He's short and chunky, a glaze of dark hair on his full-arched chest, his heavyweight ram flopping between his solid thighs, his asscheeks trim and tempting. He douses himself beneath a spray, and Hank leads the others in jumping him. There's a lot of laughing and cursing as they dogpile him to the floor, but it's suddenly quiet when someone calls "sex-play!" It's against the rules to talk during sex-play.

I cut out to the drying room, and the warm air sweeps over me, along my spread arms and legs, into every curve and hollow of my body. There's no sound from the showers, and I know the guys are crawling all over each other, sucking, fucking, whatever. Something's bothering me! I could be in there, screwing Hank, humping Nick's face or butt, blasting load after load with the gang.

But not this time.

I go to my locker and pull on my off-duty uniform, the loose-fitting shirt and trousers, the scruffy shoes. One uniform for work, one for off-duty—that's the rule. I grope my crotch and feel the ready fullness of my prick beneath the cloth. I need some all-out action. Hell, why not try the Republic-sponsored Social Center. There are always plenty of strangers looking for the same thing I am.

I leave the building, and I spot the blond across the empty flashway. I've seen him before, staring at me, even following me to the multiunit where I live. He's wearing an off-duty uniform like mine so I can't tell much about him, but he looks to be about my age and height. I'm going to find out what he's up to. I cross the street and face him.

"You've been bugging me," I growl. "What do you want?"

"You." His teeth glisten in a sure smile. "Hot and heavy sex-play." He lets one hand graze the front of my pants, as if he already knows what I've got waiting inside. "Your body, your cock, your balls, your ass—all of you, pal."

QSFx2

This sonofabitch isn't wasting time. He's good-looking, and I wonder what's hidden beneath that baggy uniform. Hell, there's only one way to find out. Yeah, I'm out to mix it up with a stranger, and this one fits the bill.

"Your place or mine?" I ask, not interested in a back-alley fast-shot.

"Mine." He clamps me on the shoulder and steers me down the walkway. "My name's Marsh, short for Marshal. I already know yours."

"What else do you know about me?"

"Everything."

We enter an area of old-time living quarters. I don't know why the Republic hasn't replaced them with total-service multiunits like the one I live in. Hell, maybe Marsh likes living without autolifts and holoscreens and all. He guides me into one of the buildings, and it's about what I expect. There's a dim-lit lobby, a male voice bellows from a side hallway, a door slams, and Marsh leads the way up a stairway—not an autolift like I'm used to.

"The guys get restless on Friday night," he explains as another howl comes from the lower floor. "They'll be cooled down by Monday."

"What happens on Monday?"

"We all go back to the Republic."

He uses a key to open a door—not a computab to activate an autoglide—and I take off my shoes as we enter. That's a rule. Marsh grins and does the same, and I dig my bare toes into the soft, nonutilitarian covering on the floor.

"Nice place," I say, viewing the large, unfunctional room. What else am I supposed to say? "Real nice."

"Make yourself at home. Drink?"

He goes into an alcove—the kitchen—and I look around. This unit is nothing like mine. Too much wasted space, clear glass windows instead of holoscreens, a couch where the autobed should be, armchairs, end tables.

"Here you go, pal."

Marsh returns, handing me a glass of creamy liquid, and I take a swallow. It tastes strange, thick and sharp, sweet and sour, mixed-up but good.

"What is this stuff?" I ask, settling into a chair that doesn't automatically contourshape.

"We call it Blow-Out." He's got a glass of his own, and he drinks, then sits on the couch facing me. "The guys here make it."

"Brewing your own booze? That's against the rules."

"We don't mess with rules."

"You sound like a Renegade," I say with a laugh, knowing the Republic banishes all Renegades.

"We wear the uniforms, take the laser tests, play good citizens." He peels off his shirt. "At home we forget the rules."

He's got a bronzed, muscled physique, golden peach fuzz covering his barrel chest, wide nipples at each side, his stomach washboard tight.

I wonder what a washboard is. Something old-time probably.

I shrug out of my shirt, matching Marsh. He views me as if he knew what he'd see, and he gets to his feet, comes over, takes my empty glass and drifts into the kitchen. I don't remember finishing my drink, but I must have. I watch the sunset glow on the sharp-cut buildings beyond the clear windows, something I've never noticed before. Marsh hands me a fresh Blow-Out.

"How come you don't have holoscreens on your windows, Marsh?"

"I'm not afraid to see the Republic." He stands there, watching me drink. "Which holoscreens do you like best?"

"The beach and ocean. Up in the mountains where a stream runs through the trees. Things I'm in the mood to see."

"In the mood to see something else?"

He takes the glass from my hand and sets it aside, opens his pants, and drops them to his ankles. His cock hangs from a tangle of pubic wire, the shaft as long and thick as any I've seen, his low-slung testicles outlined behind it. He grips the back of my neck and draws me forward. I sink from the chair to my knees, and my face floats to his crotch. I inhale the lush scent of maleness, and my tongue laps his meat. I take it into my mouth, and it throbs and stiffens. It's a real choker, but it slithers into my throat. I gulp on it, and he jerks away and hauls me to my feet.

"Something wrong, Marsh?"

"Strip down." He stoops to get out of his trousers. "We're going one-on-one, pal."

I feel like I'm dreaming, but I know this is real. I slide out of my pants, and my swollen dick snaps forward. Marsh grins and locks his arms about me. We grind together, naked and aroused.

"Let's do it." I wrestle him to the floor. "Sex-play!"

"You're a real tiger," he says. "Just like I knew you'd be."

"No talking. You know the rules."

"We aren't in the Republic, Tiger. We're on that holoscreen beach you dig."

He's right! We're lying on sparkling sand, just the two of us. I turn my head to watch the churning breakers slam on the shore and send swirling foam toward us.

"Man!" I exclaim, no longer bound by the rules. "This is great!"

"It's only the beginning, pal."

Marsh runs one hand over my chest, and his fingers leave trickles of fire and ice on my skin. He strokes my torso, and I groan with pleasure as he grips my rigid cock and slides down to it. He takes the crown into his mouth, the shaft, all the way to the base, and he toys with my churning balls.

"Marsh! I'm getting too close!"

He pulls off and stretches out beside me again, and I gulp for air, not wanting this sex-play to end, not wanting it ever to end. He slides one arm beneath my head and raises me, and he holds a glass to my lips. I swallow more Blow-Out, and suddenly we're inside another holoscreen, the woods by the stream, warm sunlight pouring through the trees, a mountain breeze washing over us.

A new sex-fire engulfs me, and I spill on top of Marsh, my face to his chest. I nuzzle the gleaming arcs. I suction the wide nipples. I lick the silk-filled armpits. I memorize his body with my lips and tongue. Shit, I've never been so all-out hot before!

"Tiger!" He shoves me down on to my back. "I want your tail!"

We're surrounded by blackness, but somehow I can see him clearly as he moves to kneel between my thighs, his blond hair glowing, his eyes blazing hungrily, his tanned physique mesmerizing. He sinks back on his haunches and empties the glass of Blow-Out on his over-sized dick. Hell, I'm no virgin, but his iron is so goddamn big, bigger than any I've ever—

Marsh raises my legs, rolling me back on my shoulders, and he presses his bulging cockhead against my tender asshole. I brace myself for the tearing shock of penetration. There is thunder in my ears, lightning flashing across my clenched eyelids.

Aggghhhh!

He inches that steel-hard ram deeper into me, and releases my legs, letting me sink to the hilt of his giant. I've never felt so filled before, as if I'm as much a part of him as he is a part of me.

"Give it to me, Marsh! I want your load!"

"You're going to get it every way there is, Tiger." He smothers me with his sweaty body, pumping steadily. "And I'm going to take yours...front and rear...all weekend long!"

I zoom to climax, and I open my mouth to howl my release—something not allowed in the Republic. Marsh covers my lips with his, feeding me his tongue, and I explode, swamping both of us with ropy spasms of cream. I'm still gushing when he bellows into my mouth...shooting his load into my guts...*Marsh!*... *Marsh!!*

As he promised, we spent the rest of the weekend together, horsing around, not giving a damn about the Republic's rules for sex-play or anything else, sleeping all over each other in a nonfunctional area called a bedroom. Too soon, it's Monday morning. We shower and shave together, and it seems strange to pull on our uniforms, ready to go to our work assignments. We tromp down the stairs and see a chunky stud coming from the side corridor.

"Nick!" I gulp. "What're you doing here?"

"I live here, leader." Grinning, he cups one hand to the front of my pants. "You should have stuck around in the showers Friday. We had some damn good gang-sex, except we had to obey the fucking rules about not talking." In spite of all the action with Marsh, I'm throwing a hard-on. "Going to move in with Marsh? Shit, he's so hot for you, he got one of the guys to sneak a copy of your compufile."

"Hell, that's against the—" I'm about to say "rules," but I've been breaking rules ever since I met Marsh. Now I know how Marsh knew all about me from the first—my compufile! I laugh and grope Nick's crotch. I feel his solid iron, almost as big as Marsh's. "Can you get me a copy of that blond bastard's file so I'll know as much about him?"

"You already know all about me, Tiger," Marsh mutters and he slaps me lightly on the ass. "Worktime, guys."

"I ended up at Hank's unit for most of the weekend," Nick says. The three of us start to the front door. "I'm going to bring him over here for a Blow-Out session. Then we'll come upstairs for gang-sex with you two. Hank's got a real hot butt, and we can—"

Nick stops talking as we leave the building. We're part of the spotless, safe Republic again. Nothing has changed, except me. Marsh walks close to me and I know he'll be waiting across the flashway tonight.

Fuck the rules!
I'm a Renegade!

Galac 19

I came alive at the Reprod Center here on Galac 19, and I was lucky enough to be charted to Senior Rank, allowing me this private domil of many rooms and a staff of slaves to do the chores and serve my personal needs. Randon is my slave master, a burly hulk who is strict with his charges and disciplines with a heavy whip when necessary. I've used him at times, and it always surprises me that he assumes the role of a slave when I mount him. On the other hand, I am Senior Rank.

So this timespan, I receive an intercom from Amus, the slaver I've dealt with from time to time. He knows what interests me, and he notes that he has an item that might be worthy. I agree to meet him, and I telesignal Randon to send a slave to wash and prepare me. Usually I drench myself in the cleansing chamber, but now I choose to enjoy the stimulation of the bath. I strip and ease into the swirling water, and the blond slave arrives, naked and muscular, slipping into the pool. He scrubs me gently—and suddenly he ducks down to take my cock into his mouth. As always, my rod begins to stiffen, and I haul him up.

"You'll drown doing that," I warn him.

"I like the taste of your dick, meelor," he says, using the correct title for one of my rank. "May I finish you off?"

"I have business in the city." I climb from the pool, and he hurries to join me, offering a tempting view of his creamy butt. He's a good fuck; I know from experience. "I'll let Randon know if I want you upon my return."

He towels me dry and attaches the strapped cup to keep my genitals secure. He dresses me in the lightweight robe, which reaches my knees, and he ties it closed with the gleaming belt of my rank. I dismiss him and descend to my autotrans. I set the omnicourse, and I relax as the machine whirs into motion. A visit to Amus is always stimulating, and my prick stirs in its restraining pouch.

As always, Amus welcomes me with a glass of Vitol, and we exchange small talk as we drink. He is tall and lean, dressed as I am, but with a sash that indicates his profession. He is sly and slippery, and I suspect that he satisfies himself with the slaves of his choice before exchanging them.

At last he telesignals, and a good-looking youth in slave garb enters. His head and face are scraped clean of all hair, and I figure that Amus is using him as a prelude to the one he expects to sell me because he knows I prefer mine to be natural. I decide to play his game, and the slave stands head-down and motionless as I remove his covering. Sure enough, his entire body had been shaved and pumiced. I run my fingers over the baby-smoothness of his chest, toy with his small nipples, stroke lower to check the heft of his organs. He is full-hung, and his denuded testicles fit into my grip. I turn him and examine his back and butt. The cleft between his asscheeks is slick, as if begging to be invaded. It might be interesting to experience sex-pleasure with him, but I do not wish to add him to my staff. I dismiss him with a shrug.

At Amus's signal, another slave enters. This one has the customary tightly clipped cap of hair on his head; but when I strip him, his body has been shaved, except for the thicket of pubic wire around his ample genitals. Amus knows I prefer heavy-cocked studs to show off to my friends, and this one fills the requirement. My prick throbs in its pouch, but I suspect the merchant is still holding back his ultimate offering. I complete my inspection of the youth and nod for him to leave.

"This is Orfo," Amus announces and motions one more young man to join us. I try to hide my surging interest.

Orfo has a cap of black hair, and he is strikingly handsome. His cloak outlines a powerful physique, a tuft of dark chest silk showing at his throat. Unlike the others, he does not bend his head but views me intently with brown-gray eyes. I wonder what he's thinking. Defiance? His rank and training versus mine?

"Orfo," I say, using his nomin in spite of his status.

"Yes, sir," he replies, not saying "meelor," as is proper. His gaze does not shift from mine.

I strip off his gown, and he doesn't flinch or waiver as I examine him. His thick neck melts into the heavily muscled shoulders, and his barrel chest is lathered with slick hair reaching to his broad nipples and downward to the crisp tangle at his groin. He continues to watch me intently as my hands roam over his sturdy torso, but he blinks when I grasp his dick. Damn it, he's got a real hammer that falls over his dangling nuts, and his meat begins to stiffen as I test it. My own ram is straining in its pouch, and I try to appear calm and indifferent, knowing Amus will double his price if he suspects I am aroused by this slave. I turn Orfo and inspect his wide back and firmly curved ass, and he tenses as I press a finger into the warm passage between his buns.

"Orfo," I whisper, wishing that my cock and not my finger was at that opening.

"Yes, sir," he murmurs, relaxing, and I order him to leave, fearing I may lose control and launch him here and now.

Amus pours more Vitol, and we begin bargaining. I enjoy this battle of wits, and I'm sure he isn't surprised when I refuse the two body-shaved slaves. He wants an astro-galac price for Orfo, and I counter that I already have my full allotment and will have to get rid of one before adding another. We spar verbally and finally strike a deal: he cuts the price in half, and I will give him a male to be replaced by Orfo. He gives me the required training history and health reports, and I read them carefully as I omnicourse my autotrans back to my domil. Orfo has been trained in all things, but he is also overvirile according to his cumscan. I plot how to bend him to total obedience.

I inform Randon of my latest purchase and instruct him to pick one of the others to be exchanged. Also, Orfo is to be isolated without any possible sex-relief but otherwise free to do as he pleases under Randon's supervision. My slave master seems amused that I call the new one by his nomin since I never have bothered to learn the others.

I return to my quarters and undress, and my pecker springs half-hard from its confinement in the pouch. Damn it, my experience with Orfo has left me youth-horny! I use the cleansing chamber and tumble onto the rest pad. I can telesignal Randon to send the eager blond to cool me, but I think of Orfo's new training, training that will deprive him of release. I switch on the sleep cycle. The lights dim, and the soothing rhythms wash over me. I wonder what it will be like to have Orfo lying next to me, ready to serve my needs. I can whack off. No, I'll wait and match Orfo's frustration when he submits to me. I drift to sleep.

At length, Randon reports to me Orfo's progress.

"He is most unusual, meelor, unlike the others. He keeps the hair on his head trimmed properly and his face shaved, and he exercises his body strenuously. But he wears garb to cover his midsection while he uses the sun-darkener so his skin is somewhat lighter down there." He wets his lips. "His prod is massive and always stiff."

"As massive as mine, Randon?"

"I am not sure, meelor. It has been so long since you allowed me to enjoy your giant." He bows his head. "Orfo has questioned me about you, displaying his warming tool openly. I believe he desires to serve you."

"Then give me time to prepare before sending him to me."

"As you order, meelor."

I use the cleansing chamber and dress in an informal robe tied at the waist with my belt of rank. No, I won't wear the cup to trap my hard-on, not this time. I sip a glass of Vitol, wondering if my plan for Orfo will work, and he enters.

Damn, I've almost forgotten how handsome he is, the crown of black hair glowing on the top of his head, his strong features freshly scrubbed, the front of his garment spread enough to show a glimpse of the dark silk glazing his full-arched chest. As before, he does not lower his head but holds his eyes on mine. Defiant? Insolent? Sex-ready? Randon has warned me that this slave is most unusual.

"Strip me," I order.

"Yes, sir."

His gaze doesn't shift, and he removes my clothing. His fingers trace over my chest and roam lower. I want him nude if he submits, and I yank off his covering. He does not react, and he gropes farther downward to touch my inflamed cock.

"Suck that meat, Orfo."

"Yes, sir."

He sinks to his knees, and for the first time his eyes break from mine. He stares at my iron and draws it to his lips. He presses down on the base and licks the tip. He holds the head and gulps on it. He inches it inward. I watch my ram suctioned into his handsome face and feel the warm wetness encircle it. The heat rises in my loins. He's a well-trained expert! He sinks back on his haunches and looks up at me. What's the sonofabitch thinking? Pride in what he's doing? Obedience? Servitude? He raises one hand to stroke my torso, and he fumbles my balls with the other. He continues with taunting slowness, perhaps knowing I'm on the brink. I grip his muscled shoulders for support.

"Orfo!" I'm blasting like a teenager on his first mission, like a liftoff from the Galac, like all-out like—

"Aggghhhh! Drink that fresh sperm!!"

He locks his arms about my hips and swallows. He milks me dry. I free myself and spill back on the sleep pad, and I watch him through half-closed eyes. He gets to his feet, naked and cock-hard, and refills my glass with Vitol.

"Shall I return to my quarters, sir?" he asks.

"You will rest here with me." I nod to the space beside me, and he eases down, his prick thrust upward like a rocket yearning for takeoff. Yeah, I'm going to break him! I finish the Vitol and my engine revives. I am prepared to continue my plan, and I stroke his heaving chest. "You are aroused, Orfo."

"Randon has not allowed me relief since coming here, sir. I have heard the other slaves sharing themselves, but I could not join them."

"What would you have done?"

"I am somewhat large, sir, so I'm usually asked to feed them my fuel front or rear. Perhaps both."

"I understand." I watch his swollen iron quiver with heat, and I know he is ready for the final step in acknowledging his total servitude to me. "Whip off your load, Orfo. I want to see you spurt."

QSFx2

He grips the potent shaft and begins to pump, his gaze still fixed on mine. His torso tenses beneath my fingers. Is it possible that his hammer is expanding even further? I cup his churning balls to demonstrate my mastery over him.

"*Sir!*" He bellows, digging his heels into the pad and arching his back.

"*Aaawwwwwhhhhhh!*"

A burst of cream explodes from his ram and puddles on his belly. Pause. Another shot, this time to his chest. Another pause. More...more...still more. No shit, he is a human volcano! He goes on erupting until he is lathered, finally slowing, finally ending.

It is time for me to continue. I shift to kneel between Orfo's thighs. I scoop a handful of sticky sperm from his body and apply it to my rigid iron. I raise his legs and fold him back to expose his pale butt. Perhaps he has kept it that way to make it a better target for my launch. I center my ram against his hole, and he reacts with a wince. Shit, he knows damn well what I am going to do! I pressure. My cockhead thrusts collar-deep. His eyes clench shut, and every muscle strains. He's tight as a virgin, so I hold there, giving him time to adjust. He relaxes slowly, but he fights a cry as I insert my tool farther. Hell, Orfo, you've been slave-trained, right? I take my time slipping my shaft deeper and deeper. The wire at my groin nests against his rear, and he groans softly as I begin to hump. Yeah, Orfo, I'm going to screw you into ultimate space!

I plow him with long, lazy strokes. I use short, sharp chops to churn his guts. I probe every quadrant of his interior. Admit I'm your master, Orfo! I start to sweat, and the droplets spatter on his upturned physique. I pump faster, out of control. He thrashes beneath me, his arms and legs clamping about me. Our bodies held together, he begins to spew a new load against my belly. I blast off, covering his mouth with mine, forcing him to take my tongue, firing my fuel into him... *yeahhh!...slave! Orfo!*

I reenter Galac 19 and free myself from him.

"You belong to me," I tell him. "Correct?"

"Yes, sir." His eyes glow. "I am here to please you in every way."

Pride? Arrogance? Something else?

I stumble to the bath and drop into the refreshing water. Orfo joins me. He washes me, then himself. I climb out, and he towels me front and rear. I return to the pad, and he follows without asking my permission. I flip on the sleep cycle. The lights dim as the gentle sounds engulf us. He molds his body to mine, warm and strong, and I slip into satisfied slumber.

Orfo is a top-gun slave. Each morning, he has my rations waiting when I come from the cleansing chamber. My quarters are kept spotless. He seems to know when I want Vitol or food or his mouth or his ass or the feel of his spurting hard-on in my fist.

I decide to reward him, so I telesignal Randon to send the blond. He arrives naked and eager. When I drop my robe, he kneels and swallows my cock. Orfo watches with a troubled frown. Yeah, he's wondering why I want another when he has serviced me so well.

"Like the cut of this sucker's ass?" I ask him.

"Want to spread those cheeks with your tool?" He blinks with surprise and nods almost shyly. "Strip and prepare to mount him."

He drops his garment. His powerful bronzed body glistens, and his prick is already stiffened. He coats his meat generously with Entrogel. He hunches behind the blond, and he aligns the nozzle of his rocket and inserts it.

I know from experience that the blond doesn't mind getting his tail blasted, but he doesn't know the size of the giant who's about to ride him. I hold his head in place, and his cry tingles against my inflamed club as Orfo inserts more of his shaft. My dark-haired slave continues his slow penetration, rubbing his palms over the blond's arched back, and the suction on my rod resumes.

Docked base-deep into the blond, Orfo begins pumping with steady, deliberate thrusts. As I suspected, he's an experienced, skilled fucker. The thick muscles knot and shift beneath his taut flesh as he increases his tempo, and he looks up at me, a full smile of pleasure spreading his lips. I can't keep from reaching down to muss the cropped hair crowning his head.

The blond is tuned to dual action. He accepts both of us hungrily, and he fists his own iron. His sperm spatters on my bare feet, hot and sticky. Shit, I can't stop my blast-off countdown. I start to unload into the slave's mouth. I clench my teeth against howling the way I do when Orfo serves me. I don't know why.

"Sir," Orfo whispers, not bellowing as he usually does when he ignites, maybe fighting the urge as I did. "Ahhhhh...sir...sir."

The three of us retro to the Galac, and I dismiss the blond. I slide into the swirling bath. Orfo joins me. He washes both of us in silence. I climb out to have him towel me, then himself.

I have one more reward for him. I bring out the chain I've had made for him, and I lock it about his neck. The polished metal glistens against the black silk at the base of his throat. He fingers it expressionlessly.

"You're the only one of my slaves to have a collar," I tell him. "Understand?"

"Yes, sir," he murmurs. "Now I truly belong to you."

We move to the pad. Orfo lies on his side next to me. I flip on the sleep cycle. The lights dim and the soothing sounds surround us. He squirms closer, one hand stroking my chest and downward. His lips nuzzle my shoulder. When we wake, I'll order him to bathe me with those lips, and when my hard-on is well lathered with his saliva, I'll launch into his ass.

His fingers enclose my prick. I grasp him.

He wears my slave chain, but I wonder if I'm not also his slave.

5 x LARS EIGHNER

Starhauler

I had never thought of a Personal Needs Device failing.

I mean, you go to the worst little johnnytrod backspace port, where the toilets don't work, where the public viewers are painted over with bobberjack slogans, where you can't tell which end of the synthesizer the food came out of, where there are out-of-order signs on everything. What's the one thing that works? The Personal Needs Devices. And usually they are even fairly clean.

You don't think of a PND failing. You plug into a PND four or five times a day. There's always one around. You take it for granted.

We were on a little one-year hop, carrying heavy ice to Algol 7. The freighter was old, junky, and patched. But it had the new sleepers. We weren't going to waveskip. The starlanes were well traveled. What's to go wrong?

Six weeks out of Algenib, the bos'n stumbled out of the Personal Needs Device, his swinging cock still hanging out of his uniform, and puked all over the place. All over the place because the ArtGrav was set to 0.15 Gs. The bos'n babbled enough before he went catatonic that we got the idea. Something was wrong with the PND.

We put the bos'n on ice and thawed Merak. It was too bad about the bos'n, but Merak is a friend of mine.

Meanwhile, the diagnostic unit went over the PND. The diagnosis was spontaneous softward virus, and the next user would have a 43 percent chance of ending up like the bos'n. And there was a small chance that the PND would actually mangle someone's cock.

I had noticed weird things about the PND for a couple of weeks. The orifice emulator seemed okay. But the imager had been giving me weird stuff. Of course the fantasy variator on the new PNDs is supposed to give you something a little bit different every time. But this one was getting way out, into stuff I'd never been close to before.

We had only the one PND. It would have been plenty since there were only six of us, and two of us were supposed to be on ice the whole time. Of course, there were the vegetables in the engine room. Come to think of it, I don't know what vegetables do, but I've never seen one use a PND.

The computer said PND failure wasn't mission-fatal and that we were supposed to see an Instructvid, number 56–40.

Merak said, "You thaw me, and the first thing you tell me is the PND is down! Whatthehell am I supposed to do with this?" He dangled his cock over his fingers, the way you do to engage an orifice emulator.

The first thing Merak likes to do when he thaws is to plug in a PND for about an hour. Merak went over and over the hardcopy of the PND's log, which, for the bos'n's experience, went something like this:

Orifice Emulator Setting: Arcturian analogous male oral.
    Imager setting: Arctuuriam same-sxe fnatassy, slave trader and cbain xoy.
    Varrritiamns O.xmb wkopth
TNK:?+sl&&&&&&&&&&vry thamtl
    FAULT DETECTED.

"No shit!" Merak said.

Merak was pissed. I was pissed. The mate was even more pissed. "Not mission-fatal, huh? Who says? Some company executive with a private fourth-generation PND right in his office, that's who. An Instructvid. What's it going to do? Tell us to meditate?"

The mate always had a negative attitude, especially about how cheap the company was. But the captain was a company man. They were about to have words. The bulkhead doors had hardly closed behind us when the captain and the mate lit into each other.

Merak hadn't dressed since we thawed him, so I peeled off my uniform and dropped it in a chute.

The mate had said exactly what Merak and I thought. We thought the Instructvid would tell us to meditate, to have cybernalysis, to do breathing exercises or some shit. Just the thought of ten months without the PND made me crazy. How long can a person go? It's something you'd never think about.

Merak and I went to a view room near the gym. I punched up Instructvid 56–40. The screen came back: "For Emergency Use Only." Then the screen locked up. We had to go through the whole clearance routine, like maybe this Instructvid was going to reveal the Q-wave secrets. I thought maybe I punched up the Instructvid for invasion by unknown aliens. I couldn't understand why all the security.

Then the naked vidguy appeared on the screen. It was the same naked vidguy who is on all the health-and-hygiene Instructivids. He's supposed to represent the average healthy human male. Except he doesn't look like a normal human male. He looks like a gung-ho cadet who has taken physconditioning four times running just for fun, and he's hung like a Denebulan stud. And he's always completely naked, even if it's the Instructvid on lowgrav toothbrushing.

So there he was, naked muscle and swinging cock, looking at us so sincerely. He smiled his obnoxious smile and in his superior way, like he's not reading a script but really is a fucking interstellar sociologist, said: "Failure of the Personal Needs Device can be stressful for individuals and can result in unacceptable strains on the working group."

"No shit!" Merak said.

The vidguy went on, "On the other hand, learning to utilize secondary or backup systems can be rewarding and an opportunity for personal growth...." and blah, blah, blah.

"Sonofabitch," Merak said. "You know, a guy like

that is plugged into one of those fourth-generation PNDs they have at the academy, oh, maybe five or six hours a day. But he's saying a burned-out PND is character building."

The vidguy said that PNDs were invented in an attempt to imitate the effects people experienced from secondary systems, and that secondary systems really occurred first and were what people made do with from prehistoric times.

I thought maybe he was going to start telling us about dinosaurs. But he only skipped back to the ancient wind mariners of Earth.

"The ancient wind mariners of Earth were often at sea for many months and even years at a time, and many of them, centuries before the prototype PNDs were operational, used the secondary system I am about to demonstrate to provide for their personal well-being..." and blah, blah, and blah.

Then the viewer went red. There were the usual warnings about how the vidguy was specially trained and we should take it easy and not sue the government if we screwed up.

Then the vidguy came back on, and you'll never guess what he did next. Never.

He put his hands all over his cock. No kidding! And it wasn't like he was washing or peeing or demonstrating some kind of hygiene routine.

I couldn't believe it. The vidguy's cock got bigger.

"It's a videffect," Merak said.

I was glad Merak saw it, too. Otherwise I might have thought I was hallucinating. Merak kept looking at the vidguy's cock on the screen and then down at his own cock.

Merak has a good-sized swinging cock. You like to be seen with a guy like Merak who is muscular and who has a cock that looks like something. You go out to some johnnytrod dive with a guy like Merak, you handle his cock a lot so people will see you are friends. Then people don't mess with you much.

But the vidguy's cock got bigger and bigger. Merak's cock looked smaller and smaller by comparison. Merak seemed to take it personally. Meanwhile, I was just amazed by the vidguy's cock.

It sort of began to stand up. Unless you've seen it happen, it's almost impossible to describe. The vidguy's cock was not only getting bigger, it was getting like—like I don't know, but anyway big and stiff and at a right angle to all those muscles the vidguy has in his abdomen.

If it was a videffect, I could not figure out how it was done. Maybe, as I have sometimes suspected, the vidguy was some weird alien with a humanoid appearance.

The vidguy said: "Although this phenomenon is imaged on some PND settings, today almost all human males are unaware of what occurs when they use a PND or what changes can occur in the human male anatomy when sexual tensions have not been fully and regularly released with PND use."

"I think he means that is what is going to happen to us!" I said to Merak. But I hardly believed it.

Merak still had a couple of fingers on his cock, and he was staring at the vidguy. "No way," he said.

The vidguy turned profile. He hung an Academy tunic on his cock, like it was a posgrav coathook. He tossed the tunic aside. His cock jumped. Jumped. It's big and still and rigid. But it's like there is a hinge or something under the vidguy's balls, and he has got control of it.

The vidguy explained it again. What he was saying was that this had been happening to our own cocks when we used PNDs. But we never saw it. And if our PND was down long enough, it would happen to us outside a PND, where we could see it.

"This occurrence," the vidguy said, "is called an erection, or more commonly a hard-on, or boner. Actually, no bony tissue is involved in the phenomenon, but you may find that hard to believe once you experience it outside of a PND. Again, this is a perfectly normal situation which is to be expected to occur in any male who does not have access to a functional PND."

That's the thing I hate about Instructvids. Most of them are a waste of time, but you have to watch them because sometimes they tell you something you need to know. If I'd got a boner without warning, I would've put myself on ice until we got to the nearest medical station.

I looked at Merak and raised an eyebrow.

"Come to think of it," he said, "I've imaged something like that before. I didn't realize what it was. You never think about imaged stuff being real."

Exactly. Imaging is so dreamlike.

The vidguy went on with his lesson. "As the word 'emulator' suggests, the orifice emulator of the PND was invented as a poor but necessary substitute for secondary systems when sublight travel meant many years of isolation for travelers. But PNDs were improved over the years. People began to prefer PNDs. And secondary systems fell into disuse.

QSFx2

"The secondary system I will now demonstrate is called masturbation, or jacking-off or a hand job."

"Hand job?" Merak repeated. "You can't tell me this guy's going to use his hand."

I looked at my own hand and thought of course not. An orifice emulator is complex hardware. No way you can do the same thing with your hand.

The viewer went red, and there were more of the usual warnings. Then the vidguy was back, and he was covering his hand with substance KA–135. He said other stuff would do, like even spit, or T–39, or even nothing at all. Then the vidguy, just in case we missed the warnings, said he was specially trained at this, and we should not do it so vigorously at first.

The vidguy started rubbing his boner. Only now he had his whole fist around it, and his hand could slide back and forth or to and fro or whatever. He moved his hand over and over his boner, and at a pretty fast clip. His hand was moving so fast I thought he might rack himself. But he didn't. So I guess he really did have some practice.

But for a while, it did not seem like much was happening. Then it hit me—the vidguy looked exactly like he was using a PND. You see guys using a PND in the public showers—in the Altair system they have PNDs right out on the streets—or maybe you plug into one of those double-orifice, double-fantasy, novelty machines they have in pubs.

That's what the vidguy looked like. In fact, he reminded me a lot of Merak when he uses a PND. The vidguy was sweating and breathing like he was in low-ox. And he turned red, all over his chest and thighs. Just like he was plugged into a PND.

I looked at Merak. His cock had stood up! Not as much as the vidguy's had by then, but because it was real and because it was Merak's, I was astonished.

"Did you do that with your hand?" I asked.

"Mostly it happened by itself."

I looked down at my own cock. It looked normal, just lying there between my balls and thigh.

Merak knew what I was thinking. "Hey, Lucky, I've been on ice for six weeks. You've been using the PND all this time. Your cock will do the same thing after a while."

I had my doubts. Merak put his hand on his cock and moved his hand like the vidguy's, only a lot slower and more gently. Merak's cock was soon much like the vidguy's, overswollen and stiff, glossy, red. And I had never realized before just how many veins are in a cock.

The vidguy began to move as if he was dancing, as if—I realized—he was using a PND. That's where I'd seen those movements of abdominals and thighs. He was not just moving his hands over his cock, he was pushing his cock *into* his hands.

Merak spit on his cock. Yeah, the vidguy had said that would work. But I never thought anyone actually would. He was moving his hand over his cock, not as fast as the vidguy, but pretty enthusiastically.

"Is it working?" I asked.

"Yeah," he said, sounding as if it surprised him, too. "It's not like a PND. But it's not bad. I think it will work."

"May I touch it?"

Merak was shocked by the question. And I guess it was pretty silly. After all, if your buddy is naked, you handle his cock whenever the notion strikes you, pretty much as if it was your own. And who thinks about asking? I guess you might ask a stranger, if he had interesting markings or maybe a real long dangler. But among friends, in a viewroom, or in the showers, or if you haven't seen him for a long time, or in a johnnytrod portside bar, your hand just naturally goes to your friend's cock and vice versa, right?

I guess I asked because Merak's boner did not seem like Merak's cock anymore. Anyway, Merak took his hand off his cock and leaned back. For the first time, I felt a boner in my hand.

It was unbelievably hard and yet somewhat fleshlike and flexible. But of course it *was* flesh, not just fleshlike. But it was not like any flesh I'd felt before and not a bit like handling Merak's dangling cock. I made a ring of thumb and forefinger, as the vidguy had demonstrated, and moved my hand tentatively on Merak's boner.

"Feels good," Merak said. "I mean real, real good."

I had been feeling something in my groin, a sort of tightness, a kind of tickle—I don't know what. I had been awestruck by the vidguy's cock and I was even more impressed by Merak's boner. By the time I looked at my own cock again, it seemed to me it was a lot larger—not hard, not a boner yet, but it definitely looked longer and thicker and it felt heavier.

Merak put his hand on my cock.

Well, naturally it feels good when your friend handles your cock, like it feels good if he rubs your shoulder or anything else. But that time, as it seemed my cock was getting larger with my every heartbeat, the feeling was good, more intense, more—what—

more concentrated in one place. It was a lot like a PND, or at least it was more like a PND than anything else I have ever felt.

The vidguy's face was all screwed up and it looked like he could hardly breathe, but he had one more line to deliver.

"We recommend...you try...this only in at least... 0.5 Gs of ArtGrav...because this...is what will... happen!" A whole bunch of stuff shot right out of his cock. But it wasn't a bit like piss. It was this white stuff.

Merak and I were so astonished that we sat there as if we were on ice.

Squirt after squirt of the stuff came out of the vidguy's cock. The vidguy took his hand off his cock. More of the stuff dribbled out. The vidguy was soaked with sweat, trying to catch his breath, and looking like he needed to lean against something.

After what seemed like a long time, the vidguy's cock appeared to be shrinking. Finally he started talking again.

He said that all guys shoot when they use the PND, but the joyhole sucks it all up and washes a guy's cock besides. So most guys never even know there is this stuff which is called semen. He says you don't want to get this stuff in your eye and it should be disposed of like all organic waste, but basically it was harmless.

Then he licked some of it off of his hand!

"Good Grus!" Merak said.

Then the vidreview started with a repeat of all the warnings and slomo shots of the key parts. The vidguy came back and said there was more to it that would be released in a month, but in the meantime we should practice on perfecting the hand-job technique.

QSFx2

The viewer went blank except for the blinking bit to tell us it was ready for another command. Merak and I were sitting there with our boners in each other's hand. I realized that I did have a complete boner, too.

It was a funny feeling. I was relieved that my boner did seem to work as well as the vidguy's and Merak's. On the other hand, I wondered why I had ever doubted any of it. Fifteen minutes earlier, it had all seemed like an Acamarian fantasy. Then there we were with boners: real, actual, matter-of-fact. However wild the idea of a boner sounds, nothing in the world seems quite as real when you have one.

"Do you think we should?" I asked Merak.

"I'm going to," Merak said. "But I wonder…"

"You know," he said, "we've imaged cocks like this, hard and big and all—"

"Boners."

"Yeah, boners. We imaged boners before we knew what they were, before we even knew there was such a thing."

"So?"

"So," Merak said, "boners turned out to be real. And the vidguy said PNDs were built originally to imitate things people did before."

"And?"

"And I think all of the things you image when you use a PND—I think all of that stuff is real."

That seemed like a weird thing for Merak to say. "What do you mean 'real'?" I asked. "It's imaging. There's nothing real about it at all."

"I mean," Merak said, "I think things on the imager are things that people really used to do before

PNDs were invented. I think people could still do all of those things, everything you ever imaged."

Merak's grip on my boner tightened. Something sticky began oozing out of Merak's boner—not the white stuff, but something clear. That was amazing. But I was more absorbed by Merak's idea. "You mean—"

"I mean," Merak said, "I think that we, you and I, can do any image we ever had. We can really do it."

I thought. I could think of only one image then as Merak rubbed his hand over my boner. It was a double-fantasy I had done with Merak in a bar, somewhere around Alhena. We had a couple of drinks. Merak wanted to plug in. He always wants to plug in.

We left our uniforms on a bar stool. Like we always do when we plug into a double-orifice machine, I had put the imager on Merak's head, and he had put the imager on mine, I hefted his dangling cock into his orifice emulator, and he plugged my cock into mine. Merak punched up an imager setting that I'd never seen before. I wish I had remembered it. I've looked for it ever since, without finding it. Merak said the setting was shown to him by a special friend.

I had punched the start button, and the orifice emulators sucked up tight on our dangling cocks.

The image—as much as I remember it, like seeing it through a dirty viewport in a fog—was set someplace with a double star. Merak was wearing a uniform of an alien kind. I'd said something—something loud, like a command, in a harsh Procyonion tongue. Merak had peeled off his violet jersey, slowly, very slowly, revealing one-by-one the mounds and valleys of his abdomen and the sparse line of black hair up his midline. He had looked especially blue-eyed and vulnerable just before he pulled his jersey up over his head—not a bit like Merak is, or at least not as Merak seems to me in reality.

I commanded him again. His big chest muscles had flattened as he raised his arms, flexing his biceps as he struggled for a moment, tangled in the jersey, and tossed it away. Then he was hopping on one foot, peeling off his pants.

Now I know what it was, but then I just imaged it: something peculiar happening in Merak's groin, his cock seeming to grow bigger. Merak stood on a rock, turned his back to me, and squatted on his ankles. I'd moved closer and closer to him. I'd admired his broad back and the imager had focused me on the way the cheeks of his ass spread.

I'd seen my hand reach for his stallion-mane, the long hair in back of the Procyon martial style. I'd grasped his hair, pulled his head back, and heard the imager mind-echoes of his bellowing as my pelvis slammed against his buttocks.

I imaged my cock going into his ass.

That had never made sense to me before. How could a dangling cock be crammed in a tight asshole? In an image, nothing makes sense; but before, I had never expected anything in an image to be possible.

A boner! That was it, of course. If I had known what a boner was, I would have known what I was doing to the image of Merak.

So it all made sense: Merak's squirming, Merak's moaning in the Procyon submissive language, the image of my sweat splashing between Merak's shoulder blades, the strange image—a tactile image—of my hands reaching under Merak and finding a bony appendage curving up his belly like a misplaced rib, the sensation from the orifice emulator of reverse peristalsis rolling over my cock, drawing me closer to Merak, sucking my cock into the image of Merak's ass.

I knew then what it was all supposed to be: the sticky, slick splashes on Merak's chest, the pressure in my cock, the pumping sensation. I was shooting white stuff into Merak's ass and his white stuff was dripping from his nipples onto the rock.

I released his hair. I felt a sense of disconnection in my cock. He had rolled over slowly and reached up to me.

"I know what you are thinking of," Merak said. His cock jumped in my hand.

"I think you do."

"Alhena Asteroid Station?" Merak asked.

"Yes," I said. Then, something I had always wondered about double-fantasy machines: "What language was I speaking?"

"Why, Procyon submissive, of course. You haven't forgotten."

"No. So you say it was I who spoke Procyon submissive?" I asked.

"Yes, yes, of course," Merak said. "I'll never forget your image, you know, as you rolled over on the rock and reached up toward me. The one thing I hate about that imager setting, it always cuts out before the final embrace. I always feel like there's something left out."

"I was on my back on the rock?"

"Sure," said Merak. "Isn't that how you remember it?"

"Yes and no. It doesn't matter. It was only an image."

"That it was. What I'm saying is, let's make it real."

We had gone to the gym, set the ArtGrav at 0.75 Gs, and found the substance KA–135 before I thought what I wanted to say to Merak. "Merak, we won't have a PND for ten months. That's a long time."

"Are you saying you don't want to do the Procyon thing?"

"Not yet. Let's walk before we try to run."

"Lucky, what is it?" Merak looked me straight in the eye. There was no evading him.

"I imaged it differently than you did."

"How?"

"I imaged *you* on the rock."

"You—" Merak stepped closer to me. My boner had begun to shrink. He took my cock in his hands, both hands, and massaged me slowly. "Does that make a difference?"

"I don't know," I said. "Let's not find out just yet."

My boner had recovered. Merak held it against his for a moment. "Amazing," he said. He placed his hands on my shoulder and pressed me down on to the bench.

Merak's fingers combed through the greasy tin of substance KA–135, leaving deep gouges in the slick gel. He stepped toward me again. I couldn't take my eyes off his cock, his boner.

Except for the crew-cut cadet on the Instructvid I'd never seen another man's cock like that: stiff, engorged, veiny, pulsing, rosy red, so hard and urgent-looking. Like my own cock.

"Please, Lucky," Merak said as he came closer.

He lifted my left arm by the elbow. He reached to my armpit with the KA–135. "This is my second-favorite image," he said with a kind of sadness and resignation in his blue eyes. His greasy slick fingers tickled as he wiped them on the sparse red hair under my arm. "I don't want to hurt you."

"I don't think this will hurt," I said, all the time watching his cock. It looked only a little bit dangerous, curving up and bouncing against Merak's abdomen.

"Now lower your arm," he said, "and keep it close to your chest."

I could see the idea was that Merak's boner was supposed to go under my arm. I turned a bit to get my knees out of his way.

"No, no. Spread your legs. I'm supposed to feel something against my legs, or I mean, against one leg. I think it is supposed to be your cock."

I spread my legs. Merak straddled my left thigh. His boner poked against my arm. Merak's cock disappeared under my arm.

"Will it work, Merak?"

"Yes. You wouldn't believe how it feels."

What an imager is no good for is the smell and the heat. As I looked up Merak's chest, my hand wrapped around my boner, just as if I'd been doing it all my life. Merak's eyes were clamped shut. His thigh pressed against my shoulder. His boner was hot in my armpit. I tried to handle my cock so it pressed against his rocking leg.

Soon the clear stuff was flowing out of my boner. Merak's leg became so slick, I could let my boner slide between the flat of my hand and Merak's hairy leg. I felt a tension gathering in my groin, more a sense of something about to happen than when Merak carefully rubbed my boner.

"It's supposed to happen to you first," Merak said.

"I don't know. It might."

"Sorry, Lucky, I've got to do this." Merak grabbed my neck and shoved against me hard. It was violent. His hips poked his boner under me with a speed I never imagined possible, like a jerking seizure. Merak's face was not like Merak's face.

"Do it, Lucky," he grunted.

I could do it. I could feel that I could make the white stuff shoot out of my cock. I rubbed my boner faster. The heat of Merak's abdomen burned my cheek.

Then I was certain it was about to happen. I wanted to see it. But Merak had my head locked against his thrusting abdomen. My boner throbbed, seeming to grow even larger and harder. I bit into Merak's belly. I was on the edge of some steep precipice.

I shot. I felt the white stuff pumping out of my boner. I heard it splatter—splatter even at 0.75 Gs—against the deck, again and again. Only at the last could I control myself enough to aim my boner against Merak's leg.

I don't know whether he felt it or whether it was like his second-favorite image. He held me tight against his thighs and surprised me just at the last by being perfectly still until I felt the surges of hot white stuff pump out of his boner, and the last lashes of his last squirts drip down on my back.

After a while, he stood back.

What was there to say?

"Can we do the last part of the Procyon thing now?" he asked.

My arm was greasy with KA-135. My ribs and back were covered with Merak's white stuff. I looked up at Merak.

I extended my arms.

October Moon

Something moved in the shadows. A rat, I thought.

But there had never been rats before and Lizbeth lay not far from my feet. Surely her young canine senses and her love of chasing things wouldn't allow a rat to get past her.

The long night was half-gone. I'd been drinking too much coffee and straining my eyes in the candlelight.

I brought the glossy magazine close to the flame. I was trying to decide which of the photographs of the smooth-bodied, sandy-haired models I wanted to shoot off to.

He had been photographed against a backdrop of summer camouflage, wearing a safari hat, a web belt slung over his shoulder like a bandido's cartridge belt, a braided leather whip, and white briefs that exposed the tip of the model's hard cock.

111

QSFx2

I squeezed my fist over my cock and flipped the pages carefully. My cock was wet by now. Both my hands were greasy.

For more than an hour, I'd sprawled with my legs spread on the sofa, playing with my cock. The candle was burning down. If I didn't shoot off soon, I'd have to feel around in the dark to build another candle from wax chips and string.

I couldn't decide which picture deserved to get my wad. The model was just my type. He was smooth and slim. Maybe a little less muscle than I like but plenty of cock—young and hard and standing upright. I wished there were more than one butt shot of him.

There it was again.

Out of the corner of my eye, I saw something move. Probably it was just a flicker of the candle, or maybe I was getting cabin fever. I'd been alone in the shack for a long time—maybe too long.

I dropped the magazine and sat up. Lizbeth raised her head, looked at me, yawned, and laid her head back down on the crocheted rug. My mind had finally got lost in my fantasies.

For many months, I'd been playing a jack-off game with myself.

The old shack was full of holes and cracks, and the window shades were in tatters. I pretended that someone watched me when I played with my cock.

I posed. I performed. I lasted longer and longer. I strained to display my cock at its fullest hard-on.

It had been only a game to begin with.

I stood and pulled up my jeans. With greasy fingers, I buttoned the fly halfway over my hard cock. I knew I would find no one outside. More than a dozen times that week, I had gotten the feeling that someone was watching me, but I never found anyone. I imagined it was one of the models with his trunks pushed down, his cock hard in his hand, and his eye pressed to one of the peepholes.

I circled the shack, but no one was there. Wind whipped loose sand through the salt grass. Barechested, I shivered in the chill of the late-October wind; the first real cold spell was due soon. The night was moonlit, but low, dark clouds rolled in ominously from the northwest.

Something moved behind me. I turned quickly but quietly. Lizbeth had ambled after me, stretching and yawning. She sat and looked up at me, as if she were wondering what the hell I was doing wandering around in the sand, the moonlight, and the chilly wind.

I didn't want Lizbeth to think I had gone nuts. My cock, which had hardly gone down, had worked its way out of my fly. I turned to the side and held it patiently until I could pee through my hard-on. My piss shot out in a high arc. I could barely hear it splash over the sound of the wind and distant surf.

Despite the cold that knotted my tits, I pulled off my jeans, perhaps to convince myself that no one else was around. I hung my jeans on my cock, just to see if I could still do it. I could, until Lizbeth grabbed a leg of the jeans in her jaws and ran back into the shack. The wind teased my hard-on, raising goose bumps on my bare ass and thighs.

I called to her to bring my pants back, but Lizbeth pretended not to hear me.

QSFx2

Something moved again.

It glided smoothly and silently down the road toward the shack, a dark figure, too small to be a car, but not a runner. I faced the road naked, my cock still standing up.

Cliff, on his bicycle—I recognized him as he saw me. He hopped off the bike and let it cruise past me and crash in the sand. He couldn't ignore my hard cock. "Is someone else here?" he asked.

"No. I'm still alone."

"Can I come in?"

I hesitated. The last time he came to the shack, he had just turned eighteen. That's why I had let him show me his body for the first time in all the years he had been coming by to talk with me. He wanted me to see his body because he had worked on it for so long. But he wouldn't let me touch him.

Cliff had flexed and posed in his briefs. He had said, "I'm not here to tease you. But if you want to get off looking at my body, well, it would be okay with me." It turned out to be more than okay with him. He had gotten a hard-on while watching me jack off. His eyes had widened as he saw me shoot all over my chest.

"You like it? Did my body do that to you?" Then he had left and not come back.

"Can I come in?" he asked again. Gently, he wrapped the palm of his hand over the hot head of my cock. "You see, things have changed."

I felt in the crotch of his shorts and found his cock hard. And I felt a revolver stuck in his belt. "I guess things *have* changed," I replied. "Come in."

Though she had been only a puppy when Cliff had

last come to pose for me, Lizbeth remembered him. She jumped up, wagging her tail, and ran to his feet. She sniffed at his boots and socks and turned away. I supposed it was jealousy when she crawled under the bed, yipping and whining.

"Come on, Bessie, don't be that way," I said. But I couldn't coax her out from under the bed.

The candle flickered out.

I sat bareassed on the sofa next to Cliff.

"I need a place to stay tonight, maybe for a couple of nights," he said. His shirt was damp with sweat.

"Why?" I asked. "What happened, and where have you been this past year?"

He felt in the dark for my cock and found it. "I'm sorry. Lee, you don't know how much I wish I'd come back, how much I wish it had been you."

He picked up my hand and put it on his shorts, over his throbbing cock. "I can't tell you why, but I need to rest." His cock throbbed. "And I need...sex with someone I can trust." Despite the cool night breeze, he was hot and sweaty.

He pulled the revolver from his belt and clunked it down on the cable spool that served as my coffee table. Then he reached in his pocket and brought out four candles. "Light one," he said.

I had electricity the last time he had visited. *How did he know to bring candles?* I wondered.

"I've been watching you for a couple of weeks. I had to be sure you were still the same," he said. I set the candle in a holder and lit it. Store-bought candles give much more light than my homemade ones. The shack warmed to the light. From under the bed, Lizbeth's eyes glowed gold. "Have you been watching me jack off?" I asked.

Of course he had. He had ridden to the shack silently on his bike. He had watched me play with my cock. And when I suspected I was being watched, his strong young legs had carried him away before I reached the door.

"You shot a lot more the time I showed you my muscles," he said.

"I'm sure it seemed that way. You'd never seen a man cum before. Had you?"

"No. And I wish I hadn't since." He stared into the candle. "Can we pretend? I've got to piss. When I come back, can we pretend it's just a week after the last time? Can we take up where we left off?"

"I'd like that," I said.

"Then put on your pants. I'll knock at the door when I'm ready." He left the shack and closed the door behind himself.

I smelled the revolver. I'm no expert, but I'd say it had been fired recently. I unloaded it on the table. There had been an empty chamber; two spent cases and three bullets rolled toward the edge of the spool. I caught one of the bullets and held it up. It gleamed brilliantly in the candlelight, a peculiar white metallic color. *Strange*, I thought.

I set the bullet on end on the table. Cliff knocked at the door. Lizbeth growled from beneath the bed, and I hurried to pull my pants up.

"Cliff," I said as I opened the door. "I'm happy to see you again."

"Hello, Lee, I"—Cliff glanced at the silver bullet

on the table—"I've been wondering if you'd like to look at my body again. You know, like last time. I've started working out again."

"I'd like that a lot."

I pushed my jeans down and sat with my legs spread on the sofa, the position I had sat in the last time Cliff visited me. He unbuckled his belt and peeled his shorts off his hypertrophied thighs. He was wearing white underwear, like the last time. His cock was already hard.

"I didn't let you touch me or see my dick last time."

"I remember. It was part of the deal."

"I'm sorry I didn't. I had to jack off as soon as I left. I must have jacked off four or five times that night."

"I wish you'd come back."

Cliff stepped closer and stood between my legs. The heat from his hard, tanned thighs flushed my face. "You would have sucked my dick, wouldn't you?"

"Yes. If you'd have felt all right about it. I didn't want to rush you."

He pulled his briefs down in front. His hard cock sprang out, almost brushing my lips. "I feel all right about it now."

Cliff's young cock at last. I'd known what it would look like—a little more than eight inches long, with an eager upward curve: heart-shaped red head; thick blue veins on an ivory shaft; and a clear, sticky dewdrop already forming at the cleft.

I sucked on his cock until his thighs quivered.

He held my head in his hands and pulled out. "I want to touch you, too, this time." Cliff stepped out of the shorts, which were twisted around his ankles.

I squeezed my cock through my greasy fists while Cliff got up on the sofa and squatted across my bare thighs. I buried my nose in his brown T-shirt between his bulging pecs. Bearing his weight on his toes, Cliff held our cocks together.

"I like your nuts." Cliff sat back on my thighs and lifted my balls gently. "Big fucking nuts," he said. "I want your big fucking nuts." He raised himself on his toes again. "Now here's a surprise."

I saw what he was trying to do. "Oh, no, Cliff, you can't."

"I did it for that monster, I can do it for a man who loves me." The hard muscles of his butt embraced my cock, and in a moment, his muscle ring opened. Cliff relaxed in my arms, impaled on my jumping cock.

"You knew I loved you?" I asked.

"No. But now I know. Fuck me. I want you to shoot in me the way you shot last time. Can you shoot that way again?"

"Not this way." I rolled us over. "Now."

Cliff's thighs wrapped around my hips. "I want you to shoot like before. Like you did. I want your big nuts."

At first he stopped me when I tried to pull off his T-shirt.

"I've got to see those muscles again," I told him. "I've got to have your hard man-tits in my mouth. Pump your chest and arms again. I've to shoot off in a man."

I pulled up the salty cotton shirt. His abs rippled with each thrust of my cock.

Then I saw across his chest the four parallel gouges, clotted with blood, fresh and purple.

He had been working out again. His smooth, round pecs flattened as he raised his arms to pull the T-shirt off over his head. I flicked one of his tiny knobby brown nipples with my tongue as my fingers felt more gouges on his broad bare back.

"Look at my arms," he said. He clasped his hands behind his head and pumped his biceps, pumped all the muscles in his body, squeezing my cock with his ring of muscle and dribbling a stream of clear lube across his navel. "Can you shoot soon?" he asked.

"Oh, yeah," I moaned.

He lowered his right arm and grabbed his cock. "Hard, Lee, fuck me hard. I can take it."

Yeah, he could take it. I probed deep into him until the bone of my pubic arch ground against his balls. He was one big, hard, flexed man-muscle, and the sweaty man-sex vapors rose from his flushed chest. Like a snake's tongue, his heart-shaped red cockhead darted in and out of his clenched right fist.

"I want your nuts, Lee. Give me your big fucking nuts!" His churning muscle rolled over my cock, and the animal thrusting took over my loins. He panted through his bared, clenched teeth.

Silver ribbons of cum lashed from his cock and slapped across his chest.

Plugged deep in his writhing muscle, I shot, spewing it into him in one long stream.

He opened his blue eyes, glinting yellow in the candlelight. "Don't pull out," he said.

"Then don't move. I can't stand it."

He saw that I was looking at the claw marks on his chest. "It should have been this way," he said. "It should have been you."

"Can't it still be?"

"I don't know," Cliff said. "I think I'll be all right. But I won't know for another month."

My cock began to shrink, but he held onto it tightly, deep inside him. My candle burned lower. Under the bed Lizbeth growled in her sleep. Perhaps we slept a little.

When I awoke, the candle had gone out. His muscle had coaxed another hard-on from my cock. I probed Cliff with the whole length of my cock until I felt his own cock stiffening between our bellies.

"Can we do it like the first time? Can I pose for you again?" he asked.

"I'd like that."

By the light of the full moon streaming through the tattered shades, I found another of the candles he had brought. I lit it. As Cliff stood up, he bumped the spool table. The bullet rolled toward the edge. I caught it and held it up to the light.

"Silver?" I asked.

"Just call me the Lone Ranger."

Cliff bent over in his first pose, the bodybuilder's crab. He looked very much like the first time, a year before, except that his cock stood free of cotton restraint. I watched him work his cock while he posed, then pulled him close to me. Pressing Cliff's rockhard shaft against my mouth, I sucked all the pulsing cum out of his cock.

And then it was dawn. He decided to go.

"You haven't had much rest," I said.

"It's better rest than I've had sleeping in almost a

year." Cliff put on his T-shirt, covering the muscles of his back and his crusted wounds.

The wind was cold. He pulled his bike upright and walked with me. By the time we reached the crossroads, the sun had cleared the horizon. We stopped by a rectangular pile of rocks on a plot of freshly turned sand.

Cliff picked up my trenching tool from beside the rocks. I had not missed it. He said, "I borrowed this early last night." He handed the tool to me.

"Who was it?" I asked.

"You don't know him. He hung around the village. He seemed all right at first. It took me a long time to find out what he was. And then a long time to find out what he wanted to do to me."

I bit my tongue to keep from saying what I was thinking.

"I know," Cliff said. "You were kind and patient with me. He seemed exciting. You must know by now how truly sorry I am."

"I know," I said.

Cliff straddled his bicycle.

"Cliff, you left the revolver at the shack. And the bullets. If they're silver, they must be worth something."

"I meant to leave them."

"Why? What should I do with them?" I asked.

"See, that's just it. You didn't understand. I don't know if it's going to happen to me. I'll be back in four weeks, when the moon is full again."

"When the moon is full," I said slowly, as if trying to recite a part of some half-forgotten verse.

"Lee, please. I have the revolver loaded. Just in case."

Cliff kissed my open mouth. Then he mounted his bike and glided away silently.

Midnight Oil

My problem was that my cock was hard and full of spunk.

Painter Hall is a dark, spooky old place, one of the oldest buildings on campus, with high-vaulted ceilings and rows of shadowy columns. All of it is dark marble and dark wood, lit as if electricity cost $100 per watt.

Painter Hall is near the center of the old campus, far from streetlights, far from everything except the old campanile. Most of the buildings around have been torn down and all that's left are the outlines of the foundation stones and the excavations made by anthropology students looking for relics of nineteenth-century college life.

I was told that in the spring couples meet in the dark recesses of the porticoes of Painter Hall. I didn't know. I had never been there in the spring. I was only a freshman.

Actually, I was a provisional freshman. We had required study hall at Painter Hall. But that night the required hours had passed. After 11:00, only the proctor and I were left in the study hall.

I was still there because of two problems. I had been looking at an integral calculus problem for a couple of hours. I couldn't figure it out, and it didn't look a bit like any of the examples in the text.

My other problem was my cock.

It was hard.

And full of spunk.

I didn't have any trouble with calculus until we got to integrals. But I'd been having the same problem with my cock all semester.

At the dorm my roommate stuck to me every minute. He went naked most of the time, and whenever I saw it his cock was about half hard. He was a swimmer and had a swimmer's build. I didn't mind looking at his body. But he said not playing with his cock was part of his training, and not playing with mine was part of his upbringing. I don't know when he went to class or when he practiced swimming. It seemed he was always around the dorm to see that I didn't get a hand on my cock or on his cock or on anyone else's.

In the gym, when I went, there was always a bunch of skinhead ROTCs hanging around in the locker rooms and showers. They had blond crew cuts, thick necks, push-up muscles, tight little butts, and swinging cocks. Sometimes I thought they hung around in the showers to get an eyeful of one another. But they talked about their girlfriends and beating up faggots.

5 x Lars Eighner

Almost everywhere I looked, I saw naked young guys or nearly naked ones. My cock stayed hard and full of spunk. Jacking off when and where I could didn't help much and didn't help for long. I tried not to think about sex. But I had built up such a load in my nuts, it didn't matter what I thought about. My cock stayed hard.

I imagined that the proctor was pissed at me. He had to stay until 1:00 A.M. if I wanted to study that long. If not for me, he could have locked up and gone home. He had been there since afternoon; he was still wearing his tennis clothes. The October night had turned cloudy and chilly. Painter Hall was as cold as a mausoleum. I had put on my windbreaker.

Only two little spots of light were left in the cavernous hall: the one on my textbook and the one over the proctor's head. All else was shadow. When all the study lights had been on, I had been able to look at the proctor's balls where they hung out of the leg of his shorts. Now everything on the dais below the desktop was black.

Against the rules, the proctor was smoking. He had brought his own ashtray and set it beside the old-fashioned cradle phone which was used for the intracampus system. He had opened a book on his desk, but he never looked at it.

One of his hands was below the desk. Tendons rippled in his arm. He might have been merely scratching his big blond-haired balls. But his hand was down there a long time.

I looked at my textbook. The integral signs looked like curly pubic hairs. My cock had got out of my shorts and was rubbing itself raw against my jeans.

The proctor rose. Maybe it was the way his shorts fit. Maybe he had a hard-on. He walked away from his desk.

The answers to the odd-numbered problems were in the back of my text. My assignment was the even problems through eighteen. I was on problem four. The proctor was right behind me. I could feel his body heat.

"Calculus?" he asked.

"Yes," I said. "I guess I'm stuck."

The proctor bent over my shoulder. I felt his breath on my neck. "A good thing that I have a math minor," he said.

He picked up my pencil. "See here." The pencil came down on the graph I had drawn in my notebook. "It has a discontinuity here. You work it in two parts."

"That solves the problem," I said.

"I don't think so." He dropped the pencil. His hand slid off the desk and onto my thigh, right over my struggling cock. "This is the real problem, isn't it?"

It had been so long. I had to gasp. "Yeah."

"I think I can solve that, too." His other hand slid under the neck of my shirt and ran over my chest.

That was when the intracampus phone rang.

It was the proctor's professor. The professor's wife was away. The proctor had to leave at once. By staying the night at the professor's house, the proctor could save his dissertation.

The proctor said he would set the thumb latch, and all would be well if I just pulled the main door tightly shut when I left. He hoped I would understand. He said he wanted a chance to work on my problem another time.

After the proctor left, I tried to stand up. It felt like there was a forty-pound weight in my groin. My balls ached.

I stumbled on the flagstone floor on my way to the men's room. I couldn't find the light switch. I made my way from one huge fluted column to the next as the full moon shone between black clouds. In the darkest moments, I couldn't see from one column to the next.

When the moon shone, I could see bats flying around the campanile. That means it won't rain, I thought. Just as I reached the men's-room door, the big bell in the campanile began to toll midnight.

When I flicked the switch in the men's room, the bulb overhead flashed and burned out. I could see only by the moonlight coming through the men's room skylight....

I bend over the lavatory to splash water on my hot, flushed face. The water feels good. I cup my hands and drink. No paper towels. I shake the water off my hands. My reflection in the cracked mirror is moonlit blue.

The pressure of the forty-pound weight in my groin pulls me down. I step into the first marble-walled booth. I don't bother to close the wooden door. I drop my pants. The toilet seat is like ice.

My cock is dangling over the water. I pee. The pain and pressure go down a little. The last of the piss dribbles out of my cock. My cock begins rising. I free my cock and balls from between my thighs, stretch out my legs, and lean my shoulders against the cold marble.

I watch my cock stiffen in the eerie moonlight. I'm going to jack off. My cock enlarges from the bottom up. My cockhead nods at the open stall door. My cock stands taller with each beat of my pulse. It gets stiffer than stiff. It bends over backward and points at my face. I wrap my fist around its base.

A cloud passes over the moon. I move my fist slowly up and down my shaft. Chances to jack off good are few and far between. I lick my palm. I want it slow and well lubed, the way that gets the most out of my nuts. I want to shoot off as much of the forty-pound load as I can.

I picture myself pointing my cock out of the stall at the last moment. The far wall is ten feet away. I might hit it.

My mouth is too dry. I just manage to make my cock moist. I milk my cock. As horny as I've been, it will lube itself soon. The moonlight sparkles on the first clear drops that come out.

The moon disappears again. In the dark, I hear the softest whisper in the low register of masculine urgency. "Psst. Buddy. Want some help with that thing?"

I thought I was alone in all of Painter Hall. The cloud passes. I see, half-hidden by the stall's door, a perfect cock-high hole in the marble partition. He's in the next stall.

I can't think why, but he must have been sitting there in the dark when I came in. I hadn't noticed him because the partitions go all the way to the floor. I suppose he's been watching me the whole time. I hope he really does want my spunk.

I close the stall door so I can get down by the hole. He's sitting on the toilet, looking at the hole. He knows I'm looking at him. He has short black hair. His eyes are blue or gray; I can't tell in the moonlight. He shaved this morning, but his face is covered now with dark blue stubble. He's young. A student. Why haven't I seen him before? I'm sure I would remember if I had ever seen him before.

He runs his tongue over his lips. It's not because his lips are dry. It's an invitation. His shirt is hung on a coathook. His chest is muscular and covered with swirls of short black hair. He leans back a little. His cock is hard. It is long and thick. His cock curves up his belly, eclipsing his navel. His low-hanging balls are suspended between his thighs. He jacks his cock.

His cock is white in the moonlight. I can see its dark veins. He pulls his foreskin behind his cockhead and, despite his enormous hard-on, he pinches his hood closed. He lets go. The skin crawls back, exposing his hard, lube-shined cockhead again.

I'm pulling on my cock. It's made enough lube that my fist glides up and down it easily.

He stands. He must be at least six feet tall. He's more muscular than I realized. His cock stands up on its own. He's as horny as I am. Hobbled by his pants wadded around his ankles, he turns slowly.

The V of his back is as perfect as I've ever seen. With a hard, quick bump he cocks his tight butt at the peep hole. He turns. Slowly his cock comes into view again. He bends. He's going to look through the hole.

I take off my windbreaker and back against the other cold marble wall. My cock bobs in front of my belly as I pull off my T-shirt. I pump my muscles. I hope he'll think I'm good enough, but then I realize that with his cock as hard as it is and the two of us alone in Painter Hall, he's not likely to leave me hot and bothered like the proctor did.

My cock surges at the thought of getting off to something besides my fist.

I turn in profile to the hole. I want to show him how long my cock is. But I don't turn my back to the hole. I don't want him to get the wrong idea.

I milk my cock. Lube dribbles onto the marble floor. His eye disappears from the hole, replaced by his beckoning finger.

"Come over here," I whisper.

"No, put it through."

"Please."

"No," he whispers. "We can't be caught. I have a jealous roommate."

Surely, I think, we're alone, and we would hear anyone coming. But I'm not going to argue with him. My cock needs servicing, and so far it seems that he's willing to take it. The question is whether my cock will fit through the hole. It barely does.

He runs his fist slowly down my cock.

A jealous roommate—that explains why I haven't seen him in the more usual places, and why he's at Painter Hall at such a late hour.

His cock had looked much thicker than mine. I thought he would never have been able to get his cock through that hole and he must know it. If he won't get in the same booth with someone else, then he must come here only to suck cock. But he's still using his hand on my cock.

"Suck on it." I whisper, but why? No one else would hear if I shouted.

His tongue flicks under my cockhead. "Take it in," I urge.

His lips run along the bottom of my cock. At last he

gets his mouth on part of my cockhead. His fist moves along my shaft between the marble slab and his mouth.

"Don't jack me off in your mouth. Take it all. Swallow it." I speak in a normal tone. In the cold marble room, it sounds like a loudspeaker.

His mouth moves violently on the head of my cock. Then nothing. His mouth is gone. His hand is gone. "Oh, no, not again!" My God, I just yelped that out loud. Not left hot and horny twice in one night. I'll cut off my cock. I'll take vows. I can't stand it.

Warm. It's not his mouth. What's going on?

It's his ass! He's spreading his cheeks over my cock. I strain against the marble. My cockslit feels the smooth skin of his hole. He pants and squirms. His hole slides halfway onto my cockhead. I thrust into the wall. "Oh, stud," he grunts. "Oh, yeah, stick it in me."

The flange of my cock slips past his muscle. Slowly his hole moves down my cock until he's pressed against the partition. I start fucking the wall. "No. Wait a second or I'll shoot," he says aloud.

My upper body pressed against the wall, my legs go slack. I try to be still. My cock's in heaven, but it wants to move. My cock throbs and surges against my will.

I picture his hard butt as he showed it to me. I try to picture it pressed against the wall, parted by my cock. He has the finest ass I've ever seen—at least, the finest one I've ever fucked. I want to see him submit. I want to see my cock stuck in him. I want my hands on that butt. I want to grab his hairy pecs. I want to handle his heavy hooded cock while I fuck him.

Except for the eight inches of my cock that are in his ass, I'm cold. My bare chest is pressed against the marble partition. My tits are as hard from the cold as they are from the sex.

"Come over here, please," I whisper. "I want to touch you."

"You *are* touching me." To prove his point he moves his muscle. Yeah. Except for the half-inch taken up by the wall, I'm touching him as deep as I can. "Okay. Now fuck me, stud buddy, fuck me!"

I fuck into the marble wall. I try to picture his hand on his cock. I can feel that he's jacking off.

"I can't help it," he whispers. "I'm going to cum."

"No. Save it for me."

His asshole squirms over my cock. I'm going to shoot soon, too. "Please, stud, please," he whispers.

My balls have tightened up. My hands find the top of the partition. I hang by my hands and slam into the wall. My cock is nearly bursting.

I grind against the stone. My body slides with sweat against the polished marble. I feel his spasms deep inside his butthole. I picture his thick cock and the hairy hard ripples of his belly.

I'm about to shoot. He squirms on my cock. My cock goes to automatic.

I'm shooting in his butthole. I'm coming in this big hairy stud and he's asshole-sucking all of the spunk out of me, the whole forty-pound load.

I freeze, my cock deep in the wall, still jumping and shooting.

"Thanks," he whispers. Painfully, I feel his hole sliding away from me. I pull out and drop to my knees. I have to have another look. He's turning around. His chest hair is matted with sweat. His fingers are pinched over his foreskin. His foreskin seems strangely swollen.

I get it. He *did* save his load for me. I stick my tongue through the hole. His foreskin bursts open.

Halfway back to the study hall, I realized I had to get his number, no matter how jealous his roommate was. I went back to the men's room. He wasn't there, though I couldn't see how he could have left without passing me.

I was already horny again. I went into the middle stall where he had been. I thought I would jack off with the part of his spunk that had missed my tongue. But his wad was gone. He must have wiped up very carefully. I jacked off with spit and left my spunk in the middle of a big old rusty stain on the wall.

For weeks I looked for him on campus. Finally I noticed a photo in a trophy case at the gym. It was a shirtless, champagne-in-the-locker-room shot. It was exactly like him, even to the exact swirls of hair on his chest, and it looked all the more like him because the black-and-white photo was turning blue, looking like moonlight. The caption said: Jack Hooten, Co-captain. National Champions—1954.

I would have said the man in the picture was the man I fucked in Painter Hall except for the date on the photograph.

It was a slim chance, but I thought the man I fucked might be Hooten's grandson.

I went to the registrar's office. I couldn't find a male Hooten of the right age in the card file of the current students. But then I thought perhaps Jack Hooten had had a daughter, and then her son would have her married name. I was stuck. There was no way to look up a student by his mother's maiden name.

The clerk in the office looked as if she could have been working there since 1954. I asked her.

She hadn't been working in 1954, but she had been a student then. She remembered Jack Hooten. After all, he was the big football star.

"But he didn't live to have a grandson. Don't you remember"—she stopped and shook her head—"Oh, of course, you're too young to remember. He was killed the year after they won the championship. Big scandal. He was shot by his roommate, the other cocaptain of the team. Right in Painter Hall. In a men's room, of all places. They said it was over a woman. Well, at any rate, that's the story they put in the newspaper."

I could see she doubted the newspaper account.

And so do I.

The Desert Inn

U could see nothing supporting the ledge, so he attributed its position high on the wall to sorcery. In fact the ledge was cantilevered, but to U that was no different from sorcery.

K'ruth began climbing the hemp ladder that hung from the ledge. U could stay on the ground or he could follow K'ruth to the perilously suspended ledge. But that was no choice at all. The ponderous bags of gold were slung over K'ruth's broad shoulders. U closed his eyes and climbed the ladder.

When he reached the ledge, the landlord's lackeys released the ladder and U hauled it up onto the ledge.

K'ruth crawled into the niche in the wall. The niche opened into a cold and clammy stone vault. From a tiny vent far overhead a little light got in through the crawl space. When K'ruth's eyes had adjusted to the dimness, he inspected the walls of the room until he was satisfied that no man could enter. Then he took the bags off his shoulders. He felt taller without the weight of the gold. He laid his sword across the bags of gold and then he doffed his clothes. In the heat of the afternoon, many of the men on the ledges went naked or nearly so. Released from its confines, the warrior's manhood sprang to life.

When he stood on the ledge again, K'ruth rubbed his shoulders where the weight of the gold had dug in. K'ruth scratched his balls and stretched. K'ruth stood at the very edge, flexing his arms and expanding his chest.

By design, none of the ledges could be reached from any of the others. But the men and youths on most of the ledges had a clear view of K'ruth. That was proved by the whistles and catcalls that echoed from the three standing walls of the archaic fort.

U wondered whether K'ruth displayed himself merely for vanity or whether K'ruth might really accept one of the offers shouted from the other ledges. K'ruth stands so near the edge, U thought. Indeed, his toes curl over the edge. A tap on the shoulder, a little shove, no more than a flick of my wrist, and K'ruth would plummet to his death. And then the gold would be mine.

But for how long? U answered himself. Without K'ruth my throat would be slit before I was out of sight of this place. The slimy landlord has spread the rumor of our wealth, as I can hear from K'ruth's propositions.

"Leave your gold with your companion; I only want that pole between your legs." "Favor me, and you'll leave with twice the gold." "I've heard Vallychian semen tastes like honey, and I've got a sweet tooth." The calls came from all sides, some in languages U did not understand.

"Help me, Vallychian stud, before my eunuchs tear themselves apart. I'll make it worth your while." U could see where this cry came from. A fat Aquekian merchant was ensconced on a nearby ledge with four round-assed eunuchs. That, U reckoned, was three more than the fat man could hope to satisfy. Indeed, the eunuchs were already pulling out one another's hair, contending for the honor of sitting on the merchant's tiny cock. K'ruth had not responded to any of the other pleas, but he chuckled at the Aquekian's plight.

The merchant called, "If you won't cum yourself, get your friend stirred up and send him over. You've got big, beautiful muscles, Vallychian, but one dick is the same as another to these wildcats. I'll pay well for a good night's sleep, which I won't get unless someone helps me plug these wanton holes."

"I'll ask my friend, but I'm afraid you're on your own," K'ruth replied.

K'ruth! K'ruth's name exploded in his skull.

K'ruth turned. On the ledge a little higher up, a Limnic priest stood in the emerald robes of his order. The priest was a very old man, but as K'ruth glanced at him the priest parted his robes to reveal a cock almost as large as K'ruth's. This must have been a mighty thing once and, though it sagged under its own weight, it still was far from harmless.

I know what you really want, K'ruth.

If so, priest, you know you're not the man to give it to me.

Alas, K'ruth, 'tis true. But I want to watch.

Here's my naked body on the ledge. You hardly need my permission.

I mean, to watch you in the stone room tonight. I see your plan. It would give me great pleasure to see your plan unfold. To my mind's eye, the stone wall is but a veil which I can draw aside at will.

If you can see whatever you will, then why ask my permission?

It's more auspicious if you agree. And I will help you. You know your friend's mind is poorly balanced and full of dangerous ideas. I can nudge him in the right direction.

I want U to choose for himself.

He will. Just a gentle nudge. He'll do nothing that is not already in his mind to do.

Very well, priest. Watch and nudge if you will. But I think you mean to do more than watch.

You're right, K'ruth. What I watch I feel as if with my own flesh.

K'ruth's cock jumped. His balls seemed to twist around each other. A drop of clear dew formed at the slit of his cock.

Do that again, priest.

K'ruth, you have a long night ahead of you. But observe what I can do with the vain thing on the opposite wall.

K'ruth looked at the ledges on the facing wall. Most of the men and youths had stripped in the heat. K'ruth had no trouble spotting the one the priest meant—a blond youth with hair like a lamb's fleece. His cock was hard and he was strutting and posing.

The gnarled, hairy men on the adjacent ledges were pulling on their cocks as they observed the youth. But the youth's cock stood of its own accord.

The youth teased the lusty brutes who were safely out of reach, wiggling his ass and spreading his cheeks and then spinning on his heels to thrust his cock at them.

K'ruth could see when the priest's mind touched the young man's cock. The strutting and the teasing stopped. The youth stood flat-footed with a puzzled look on his face. Soon the youth was red and gasping. He stared at his cock as if it were a scorpion.

The young man's red cock began to ejaculate. The youth was more than surprised, but he thrust his hips as if he had meant to be shooting his wad off the ledge. It did not stop. The youth stumbled backward and lay on the ledge. His cock squirted white fluid onto his chest and his belly. Then the fluid was clear. Then the youth's cock twitched like a drunk with the dry heaves. The youth lay moaning and rubbing semen over his body.

"I suppose it was the sight of you that did that to him," U said sarcastically.

K'ruth grunted. He glimpsed the priest again. The priest was wiping his cock with an emerald cloth.

"So what are you planning to do with that thing?" U could only have meant K'ruth's fleshy scimitar.

"Don't you have some plan for it yourself?" K'ruth asked.

"Think again, K'ruth. For all your muscles, you'd still be in that hellhole prison if my ass had not found the way out. So you saw a few guards fuck me, and you saw me act like I enjoyed it. So what?"

"If that was acting, U, you're very good at it."

"Remember, K'ruth, every man who fucked me in that prison now has a new mouth—the one I cut for him beneath his chin."

K'ruth and U turned to spy the source of a hollow, sickening shriek. One of the eunuchs had lost the battle for the merchant's cock. The boyish squeals continued until the eunuch struck the ground.

"What a shame to die fighting over such a tiny cock," U said.

A boy beneath their ledge hailed them in a language that U did not know. K'ruth spoke it, however, and there was a brief exchange. K'ruth let down a line, and the boy attached a basket to it. K'ruth hauled the load up quickly and dumped the basket of wood and live coals into a bowl-shaped depression in the ledge.

There was another bowl carved in the ledge, but it had a hole in the bottom. U asked what it was for.

"You shit through it," K'ruth said.

"Then why isn't the ground under the ledges layered in filth?"

"That you'll see for yourself soon enough."

"And why hasn't someone removed the eunuch's body?"

"The answer to that is the same," K'ruth replied.

U opened the packet the landlord had given them. The bread was black and hard as stone. The salted meat was vile and wormy. The cheese smelled like a goat, but it did not taste so bad. The wine was strong, and there was plenty of it. U dropped the bread and meat through the shithole, and they supped on the cheese and wine.

U observed that K'ruth's cock was as hard as ever. "Why don't you take that where it's wanted while there's still light?"

"I wouldn't dream of leaving you," K'ruth said.

You mean, U thought, you wouldn't dream of leaving the gold.

The old fort had once had four sides. Clearly it had been built by some ancient race, far superior to the present degenerate proprietors. And it must have been built as something more than a desert way station. There had been two short, narrow walls and two long, broad ones. One of the short walls had been reduced to rubble in some forgotten battle, which seemed to indicate that the fort had once contained something of value.

As the sun set, the livestock and the rabble, riffraff, and retainers who could not afford accommodation on a ledge gathered against the remaining short wall. Planks were removed from the ground, revealing a trench running parallel to the remaining short wall. When every living thing on the ground appeared to be across the trench and within the walls, the last of the planks were removed. Several large casks were breached and their oily contents spilled into the trench. When it was quite dark, a torch was tossed into the trench. Flames spread from one long wall to the other.

"Surely the night is warm enough as it is," U remarked.

"You'll see," K'ruth said. "In fact, here they come."

Three of the things were already picking their way over the remnants of the ruined wall. Then there were four—then a dozen—then a score. When the first of them reached the eunuch's corpse, they gave out an unearthly cry. Soon the multitude of slimy, smelly things were bellowing and chirping. The flesh did not remain long on the eunuch's bones.

"How can anyone—any thing—live like that?"

"Take a whiff," K'ruth said.

U inhaled and almost vomited. The air had putrefied.

"They don't live like that. They don't live at all."

"It's ghastly. Look, they are breaking the bones to get at the marrow." U shuddered.

"Don't stare so long at the dead. Give some attention to the living." K'ruth brushed his cock across U's thigh.

"Have I a choice?"

"You wouldn't enjoy it?"

"I never enjoy it. I told you. I use my ass for strategy."

"Then think of this as strategy." K'ruth wrapped his arms around U's shoulders. "Three years I labored in the prison mines of Eckta, chained to the rock face by day, at night locked in a solitary cell. We've been on the run since we escaped. I destroyed the caravan to get the gold. Whoever owned it may be looking for us. More than three years I've had nothing to fuck but my fist, and I do not know when we can stop again." K'ruth flexed his arms, trapping U's breath. "You'll find it strategic to please me. I don't care whether you enjoy it."

"I see." U ducked under K'ruth's arms. Very well, Vallychian, U thought, tonight you fuck me and maybe tomorrow, too. But one night when you roll off me and fall asleep, you won't wake. You'll be deader than the things below us.

U loosened his garments.

"No, leave your clothes on. I'll rip them off."

"Too late to rape me. I've agreed." For the moment, U thought.

"It must look like rape. I have a strategy, too."

"Yes?"

"Word is out that we've got gold. Some of these

swine would gladly risk their lives to get the gold. I want them impressed that I might do worse—if they tried—than kill them. You must act as if you hate it."

"That won't be acting."

"You must let them know it hurts."

"That will pose no difficulty. Your cock's twice the size of anything the prison guards could muster."

"Then we begin."

K'ruth threw U onto his back. U screamed. In an instant, U's trousers were shreds.

"I can't take it! By the gods, it's too big!" U shrieked.

No one on the other ledges was watching the horror below. They watched the enormous shadow of K'ruth's cock part the shadow of U's ass. "Fuck him, Vallychian! He's got it coming."

"Screw him into the stone!"

"You wouldn't have to wrestle so to get it in my ass, Vallychian."

"Fuck him for me. Fuck him hard!"

U's shriek turned to a scream that made the ghouls shudder. "Pull it out, K'ruth—it's too big—it'll kill me!" Then U whispered beneath his teeth, "I'm not acting, you pig! Take it out."

K'ruth whispered back, "Don't let them know it's over."

"Over?" Yes, it was over. U felt the Vallychian cock shrinking. "You dumb ox. Don't you know I want it now? And you're as useless as a side of beef. A *stinky* side of beef, I might add."

"I told you it had been three years. You said you wouldn't like it anyway. Remember to scream." K'ruth backhanded U. U screamed.

Help me, priest.

What? Already? Your plan for the night is not half-done.

Make my cock hard again before it slips out of this gaping hole.

Easily done. You'd get it back in a minute, anyway.

K'ruth thrust his hips tentatively. The motion passed throughout U's body. "Good, K'ruth," he whispered. "Now fuck me and don't stop."

"As long as you keep screaming."

"Aiyeee!" U screamed. U shrieked. U begged for mercy.

The moons rose.

The leering rogues on the other ledges shot their wads, and shot their wads again, and chirping ghouls licked up the man-juice that splashed off the ledges. But at last, no matter how pitifully U screamed, only K'ruth's cock was still hard.

The other lodgers were weary of it.

"Enough is enough, Vallychian!"

"For the gods' sakes, pull out of the lad if you can't cum."

"I offered you my ass and gold, Vallychian, but now I swear I'd rather feed my flesh to the ghouls below than get the kind of dicking you're giving that one."

"Have mercy on our ears if not his ass!"

"Had enough?" K'ruth whispered.

"I could go on, but I'm getting hoarse. Are you going to cum?"

"I told you when I came." K'ruth pulled out. "Now weep."

U wept. It was not difficult. K'ruth's cock left a vacancy. U sobbed loudly, then more quietly. There were no more moans or gasps from the other ledges.

Even the corruption on the ground was quiet. K'ruth seemed to sleep. His cock was still hard.

U got up and squatted over the shithole. The things on the ground chirped in anticipation and vied for position under the shithole. U was disgusted, but he had to shit. There was no mistaking the squeals of delight from below.

When U reached into his pack, he had not quite decided whether he was looking for his dagger. The plan formed in his mind by pieces. Some pieces fit; others did not.

After such a rape, no one would blame him if he killed K'ruth, not that blame would count for anything in this place. Slit K'ruth's throat silently. Prop him up on the ledge, like he's napping. Yes. Do not throw his body to the ghouls. Make him protect me, even after he's dead.

Take most of the gold out of the bags. Fill the bags with stones and put a few pieces of gold on top. Leave the bags in plain view on K'ruth's lap. The rest of the gold…in my pack, in my codpiece, elsewhere in my clothes. I have to pretend it is weightless only long enough to get to the horses.

The gold is mine, anyway. It is only a fraction of what K'ruth promised me for showing him the way out of the prison maze.

If they see the gold on K'ruth's lap, no one will bother me. I'll have to leave the ladder down. But they'll think K'ruth is napping, and no one will dare go up for fear of disturbing him. I'll bribe a stableboy—not too much; he must not know I have the gold. There are two of them. I'll suggest the one I bribe can blame the other. I'll take K'ruth's horse, too. By alternating horses, I'll soon be beyond the reach of anyone here.

Then what? Hire mercenaries. Make sure they hate one another. Play them off against each other to keep them from conspiring. And hire lads for my pleasure, like the fleece-haired one who came so much this afternoon. A palace would not be beyond my means.

As U's fingers closed on the hilt of the dagger, his wrist was caught fast in K'ruth's hand, hard as an iron manacle.

"Drop it," K'ruth said. "Be quiet and crawl into the niche."

"So you can murder me in there?"

"If I wanted to murder you, I'd drop you off the ledge right now and leave your body to the ghouls. Crawl into the niche."

U crawled into the niche. He had gone a long way in the darkness before he discovered he had entered a room. He stood. He saw a faint red glow in the darkness. Then K'ruth touched the firebrand to the torch.

"Now take off the rest of those rags," K'ruth demanded.

K'ruth had only ripped off such of U's clothes as had been necessary to consummate the rape. Now U removed the rest. U folded his arms across his chest. U had no reason to be ashamed of what hung from his groin, but he wanted to avoid a comparison with the Vallychian's massive hairy chest.

"Lower your arms and let me look at you."

U reddened. The prison guards had only wanted to see his ass.

"'Tis true, you're no warrior. But your chest is smooth and hairless. You've got enough muscles to cover your bones. Your balls are big and heavy. Your belly and your ass together are not as wide as your shoulders. Your thighs are lean and hard. I like what I see. I imagine you as a young athlete."

You were in prison too long, U thought.

"Come here," K'ruth commanded.

"What for?"

"So I can lick your balls and suck your cock until it gets hard."

U hesitated. The Vallychian's cock was still hard.

"If I meant to rape you again, I'd have done it on the ledge and given our friends another example. Come here." K'ruth knelt.

U took a step toward K'ruth and then another. Then it struck him: there's every chance this hulking brute really wants to suck my cock.

Suck. Yes, K'ruth sucked. Sucked him as if he had a thousand tongues and no need to breathe. Don't stop, U thought.

But K'ruth drew his mouth away. In the flickering torchlight, U's cock glistened like a long, hard jewel. "Perfect," K'ruth said. "Now get my sword."

U did as he was told. The sword was heavy. Obviously, K'ruth could take it back whenever he pleased.

"Now strike me with it," K'ruth said. "The broad side."

K'ruth had bent onto all fours. U's target was plain.

"It's what I want," K'ruth said. "Do it."

U swung the blade. U wondered that the sword did not shatter, for K'ruth's buttocks seemed hard as stone.

"Again!" K'ruth cried. "And this time put your back into it."

U thought the sword rang when it struck K'ruth's butt.

"Ow! Ow! Yes, that's it. More of that. As hard as you can."

U's arms grew sore. K'ruth's ass grew red. One of K'ruth's hands disappeared, but U could guess where it was at work. The sweat washed in sheets down the tense muscles of K'ruth's back. At last U could hold the sword no more. Tiny crimson ribbons crisscrossed K'ruth's ass.

"Now fuck me!" K'ruth moaned. "Stick your cock up my ass!"

In truth, U's cock had somewhat subsided from the exertion, but it revived at once. U was convinced K'ruth wanted it. U took hold of K'ruth's shoulders as if to turn him over.

"No, not that way. Take me like an animal. Mount my butt."

U's cock blunted itself against the Vallychian's hole. The massive body twisted. K'ruth raised his head and bellowed.

K'ruth gasped, "I'm almost a virgin, and your cock's as big as mine. Hurt me however you must, but get it in."

U took aim and shoved. It was driving steel into stone, but bit by bit, U's cock disappeared into K'ruth's bowels. "It's in," U reported when his balls lay at K'ruth's hole.

"Fuck me!" K'ruth growled. "Fuck me!"

"A moment. I've been in prison, too."

"Before prison, when did you get in a warrior's butt?" K'ruth hissed.

"Never. Never anything except a temple prostitute or two."

"Then fuck me, fool. Fuck me!" *Help him, priest. It's too late for me, K'ruth.*

K'ruth's mind filled with the picture of the priest's cock, standing up like a young man's. The priest's cock spewed fire and sparks into the inky darkness surrounding him.

K'ruth felt U's cock move within him. "Yes. More of that. Fuck me."

"I can't last long, K'ruth."

"Then deep, get deep."

U drew his cock out almost full length and plunged into K'ruth again. "Oh, yes!" K'ruth moaned.

U's balls jumped. He did not dare try that again. Instead, he pressed deeper. In and in, he dug his nails into the round muscles of the Vallychian's chest—hard and brawny they were, the same stuff as the Vallychian's buttocks, and like K'ruth's buttocks, K'ruth's breast was soon ribboned in scarlet.

U coiled his belly, pressing deeper—by the gods, if he had twice the cock, he could not get as far into K'ruth as he wanted. U strained as if he were shitting a stone. K'ruth's hole snapped as if it would snatch U's balls, too.

U smiled. He was ready to fuck K'ruth.

K'ruth squirmed. "You animal!"

U fucked. His balls slapped on K'ruth's stony butt. U grunted. K'ruth growled.

"How long shall I fuck you, Vallychian? Oh, how I love to run my fingers through the hair of your belly and feel my cock poking you in there."

"Don't crow yet, U. How long do you think you can last once I mean to make you shoot?"

K'ruth's bowels seized U's cock and began to milk it.

"Aiyee, K'ruth, you'll get my wad."

"Drive it in deep."

U's cock plunged into K'ruth's gut, deeper, and then deeper still. There U's wad splattered like a ripe tomato against a stone wall. "Gods, K'ruth..."

"Leave it in as long as it will stay."

When U's cock fell out of K'ruth's butt, K'ruth stood. K'ruth stroked his slick cock. "Give it to me," U begged.

"No, you must see it. You must watch." K'ruth's cock glinted with the oil of male desire. "Squeeze my nuts."

U caressed K'ruth's swollen balls.

"Squeeze! Squeeze as if to crush them. In prison I'd use stones between my thighs. Squeeze hard!"

As much as U squeezed, so much did K'ruth's cock swell.

"Squeeze harder!" K'ruth's fist flew on his cock. "Have you ever seen a man so aflame as I am now? Have you?"

U had not.

"Then squeeze, damn you, squeeze!"

U squeezed. Surely no man save K'ruth could stand such treatment. But the Vallychian's balls withstood it, and the pressure seemed to fire K'ruth to ecstasy.

"Bite this!" K'ruth pressed U's mouth against the wall of flesh that was K'ruth's chest.

U bit into K'ruth's hairy hard brown nipple. It tasted of the flood from K'ruth's armpits and of red metal.

"Yes. It's almost there. Bite. Squeeze. Nearly. Oh, gods, yes! Now quick, look at my cock!"

U tore his teeth from K'ruth's nipple. K'ruth's cock was as hard and glossy as polished steel. K'ruth dropped his fist. His cock jumped.

As fast and hard and as much as drunkard's piss,

K'ruth's white juice flew from his cock in an arcing stream.

K'ruth's balls twitched in U's hand. After the stream, the pulsing wads shot.

The stuff covered K'ruth's clothes, K'ruth's sword, and the bags of gold. Still, there was more than enough left to fill U's mouth, though U had to suck for the last of it.

After a while, when they were a sticky pile of flesh on the stone floor, U said, "I've never seen anything like that."

"Well, there was the youth on the ledge," K'ruth reminded. "But he was enchanted."

Later U asked, "Now, what?"

"Now I sleep. And then you'll want to fuck me again. And at dawn, if you're willing, I'll rape you again on the ledge."

"That would be nice. But you'll sleep? You'll sleep after you found my hand on my dagger?"

"Why not? Now that you see my point?"

"What point is that?" U asked.

"Oh? Perhaps I'd better not sleep after all."

"Explain."

"As well as you can, I can figure a dozen ways you might kill me and get out of here safely with the gold. Then what? You'd hire mercenaries to protect you and lads for your pleasure. But I can protect you better than a mercenary. You saw what I did with the mercenaries who were guarding the caravan. And I don't think you can buy better than my ass. Tell the truth: Am I wrong?"

"No. You're right about that."

"Then you see, you're better off having me and the

gold than having just the gold and spending it to try to replace the services you have from me."

"No doubt about that."

"So that leaves you only one reason to kill me."

"I can't think what that would be."

"That you'd think you were useless to me. Once you led me out of the prison maze, you thought your usefulness was at an end. You certainly were more of a liability when we attacked the caravan. You'd think it only a matter of time before your uselessness was apparent to me. So you'd plan to get rid of me before I did the same to you."

"Yes. There is that."

"So I can assume your mind's at ease," K'ruth said.

"Not quite. I still don't see what you need me for. Or at least, why you might not replace me with any number of others."

"Oh, that. You saw how I enjoyed myself tonight."

"But anyone could have done as I did."

"Not anyone. It's my real pleasure and only the third time in my life I've had it. What man could I turn my back on while he held my sword? And if I could trust someone else not to destroy me in my secret pleasures, how many of them would hold their tongues? One whisper of my secret would quite undo the impression your rape on the ledge was meant to create. Everyone would think I was the same man when I held my sword as I was when you squeezed my balls. I'd show them they were mistaken. But having to prove the point again and again would soon grow tiresome. I can trust you to keep quiet. You see, my reputation protects you as much as my sword does. If you bragged you fucked K'ruth and crushed his balls, you might as well be begging to have your own throat slit as well."

U thought about this for a long time. Then he said, "I see."

But K'ruth was snoring.

The Trade

It's really too early in the day, Bruce thought.

A fly buzzed around the Dumpster at the corner. In the August heat, the Dumpster stank. Bruce peeked around the corner. The trade was still there, leaning against the wall near the entrance of the alley.

He sure looks like trade, Bruce thought.

Bruce had walked past the man twice. *I should make my move or forget it*. Bruce walked slowly toward the man. Bruce slowed even more as he came near the man—the man with the hard hat, the athletic T-shirt, the greasy jeans.

The man was not going to speak first. Bruce was almost past him.

"Got a light?" Bruce blurted out, too suddenly.

"In the alley," the man growled as he grabbed Bruce's arm.

Bruce pulled back instinctively from such a violent move. It made no difference. The man was much stronger than Bruce. Bruce was dragged into the shadows far down the alley.

"Look, how much?" Bruce asked. "I don't have much money at all."

"You know how to suck dick?"

Bruce didn't know what to say.

"Hey, it's free. You don't have to pay me," the man explained. "But, like, I'm straight. I don't do nothing back."

Bruce nodded.

The man's hand closed on the back of Bruce's neck. "Well, get to it. I got a dick that will change your life." The man's hand pushed Bruce to his knees. The man's button fly was just an inch in front of Bruce's face. Bruce unbuttoned the man's fly.

When the man's cock was free of his jeans, Bruce scarcely had time to look at it before it was forced into his throat. It was big, rockhard, and shiny. *Not*, thought Bruce *so great that it's likely to change my life. Straight men are so vain about their dicks.* But it was good hard cockmeat, and the man was hot and forceful without hurting Bruce.

Bruce tried to get a hand free to open his own fly. But the man was already pressing Bruce against the wall. The man's powerful legs were driving the hard, hot cock into Bruce's mouth, fucking Bruce's mouth. Bruce could move only just enough to rub his dick through his jeans.

Already the man was gasping and grunting. Bruce wanted to make it last, but he could not move.

"Here's my nut, cocksucker," the man said between his teeth.

Bruce's mouth was flooded with hot, sour cum. His own cock throbbed, and a sticky stain spread down the right leg of his jeans. Bruce swallowed. He swallowed again and began licking the man's cock tenderly.

"That's it, cocksucker. You got it all." The man pulled his cock out of Bruce's mouth. "I don't do nothing back."

"That's okay—" Bruce was about to explain that he had cum in his pants.

"Don't matter whether it's okay. I don't do nothing back. I'm straight. Hey, cut it out. None of that love shit!"

Unconsciously, Bruce had laid his cheek against the greasy jeans on the man's thigh and had begun stroking the man's flank with his dry hand. None of the trade had ever objected to that before. At least not in the minute or two after they had cum.

The man stepped back, out of Bruce's reach. He milked the large limp cock a couple of times, but there wasn't a drop left in it. "See ya around, man. I gotta fly."

And then the man was gone. Bruce sat on his heels for a long time, leaning against the wall. *I have got to stop doing trade*, he thought. *That one could have killed me as well as anything.*

Bruce snapped back to reality when a fly landed on the huge cum-spot on his jeans. The spot spread from halfway down his thigh almost to his knee. There was no way to cover it up. Bruce just had to hope that no one would notice before the stain dried in the August heat. He shooed the fly and stood up.

Alan looked out the window. A September storm was

brewing over the bay. There would be just enough time to get to the gym before it started to rain. Already it was dark enough so that Alan could see his reflection in the window. Alan forced a smile onto his face.

"Bruce, come on. Let's go to the gym." Alan bounced into the living area wearing his chartreuse silk gym shorts, a blue and green soccer shirt, and his green Reeboks.

"You go ahead. I don't feel like it."

Alan looked at the TV that Bruce was watching. "You said that the last three times. It's not like you."

"It's just so boring working out. And I hate the smell of the gym."

"I don't believe my ears! What's wrong, Bruce?"

"Nothing. Get out of the way. I can't see the TV."

"Something is wrong. You say it's boring to go to the gym. You say you don't like the smell of the gym. You haven't worked out in two weeks. Come to think of it, you haven't made love to me in three weeks. And look—here you are, watching commercial television. Is the cable out of order?"

"No. The cable's working fine. I just happen to like this show."

"You like watching *The Wheel of Fortune*?" Alan reached to feel Bruce's forehead. "Are you ill?"

Bruce realized that he had pulled back involuntarily to avoid Alan's touch. Bruce looked puzzled for a second. "No. I'm fine. I never felt better."

"Fine? The perennial hypochondriac? Bruce, you used to give someone a medical history if they asked, 'How do you do?' Now you tell me you're fine. You've never in your life said you were feeling fine."

"Well, now I feel fine. All right?"

"Bruce, I think I better take you to see Dr. Jim."

"Hey, I don't need a doctor."

"Yes. Yes, Bruce, I think you do."

"Okay! Okay! If it will get you off my back. Jesus, I can't take this constant bitching. Now get out of the way. I can't see Vanna White."

"Yoo-hoo! Anybody home? It's Mona." Mona peeked through the door at Bruce and Alan's tasteful living area. Mona coveted the Picasso sketches although, as Alan always explained, they hadn't been so very expensive.

"Mona? Come on back. I'm in the kitchen."

Mona entered the apartment. He found Alan rolling croissants on the marble slab. Mona sat at the bar. "Mind if I have a drink?"

"Oh no. Help yourself. Oh, let me get you some ice."

"Never mind. I don't need it." Mona poured four ounces of rye into a highball glass and downed it, Alan noticed. That drink seemed a little excessive, even for Mona. Alan shooed a fly away from a buttery corner of the slab. "Is something on your mind, honey?" Alan asked.

"Yes, well. First let me ask you. How are things between you and Bruce?" Mona poured himself another rye, but he seemed content to sip this one.

"Not so good, now that you ask. Why do you ask?"

"Honey, darling, dear. I don't want to be the one to break it to you. I don't know how to soften the blow. I was downtown in high drag, you know."

"Yes. Go on." Alan put down the rolling pin and looked at Mona. Mona had not quite managed to get all of his eye makeup off.

"You'll think I'm just flattering myself."

"Out with it, Mona."

"Your husband tried to pick me up." Mona downed the rest of the drink and poured himself another one. "You don't seem to be especially surprised to hear that."

"I'm not especially surprised to hear that. He hasn't touched me in weeks. And he's been doing all kinds of strange things.... Oh, my dear, I didn't mean that the way it sounded."

"No. Strange is right. I told you I was in high drag. The strange thing is, he didn't recognize me. I almost think..."

"What? Go on."

"It sounds crazy. I almost think he thought I was an RG."

"A real girl?"

"Exactly."

"Hmmm."

"Alan, what does it mean?"

"I don't know, Mona. I thought he was ill. We're supposed to go back to Dr. Jim's this afternoon for the results of the tests. Pour me one of those while you're at it."

The front door slammed.

"What in the hell is this shrieking?" Bruce bellowed from the living area.

"What shrieking?" Alan called.

"This goddamn shrieking on the stereo."

The sound of a needle skating over a record came over the kitchen speakers; and in a moment, from the living area, the little snap of vinyl bent past the breaking point.

"Oh God, Mona," Alan whispered. "It is—it was *Don Giovanni*. His very own record. His favorite."

They had been in the waiting room for a long time when Dr. Jim came to the waiting room. It was part of Dr. Jim's person-to-person style of medical practice that he came to the waiting room himself.

"Bruce," Dr. Jim called. "And Alan, you'd better come, too."

Bruce and Alan followed Dr. Jim, not to an examining room, but to his office. Alan was surprised to see another man waiting for them.

"Bruce and Alan, this is Professor Tom. I asked him to join us. There are some things I want him to explain to you himself."

"A professor? Professor of what?" Alan asked.

"Of a kind of biology," Professor Tom replied.

Alan looked suspiciously at Professor Tom. "What kind of biology?"

"Professor Tom is a virologist," said Dr. Jim.

"A virologist? Then it is—"

"No. It's not any of the sexually transmitted diseases we tested for." Dr. Jim tried to look reassuring, but it was the piercing blue-eyed, encounter-group stare that always put Alan's teeth on edge. "Professor Tom, why don't you take over."

"Oh yes. I need to know if the two of you have been completely monogamous. It's important."

"Yes," said Alan immediately.

"Well, practically," Bruce said slowly.

"Practically?" asked Alan.

"I thought so." Professor Tom laid out a series of photographs on the desk. They looked like pictures of pairs of strange, banded kinked-up snakes. In each picture, the pairs of snakes were numbered 1 through 22, and then there was a pair of mismatched snakes. "These are chromographs. They show pictures of a person's genetic makeup. This one is from an old sample from Bruce. This is Alan's current sample. This is Bruce's current sample. And these are from a group of completely heterosexual men, each of them straight as a board. Now, see this little bump on the X chromosome of Bruce's current sample, and over here on the control group we—"

"Skip the shit!" Bruce said. "Give us the bottom line."

"You see I've been working on this theory—"

"I said skip the shit."

"I think you've caught a retrovirus of a kind we've never seen before. Your genetic makeup is being altered. It's a million-to-one shot, but it's being altered in a way that produces an extra kink on the X chromosome. Otherwise we wouldn't have a clue as to what was happening. You see I've been working on the theory—"

"I said the bottom line. What's happening to me?"

"You're developing an extra kink on your X chromosome. It looks very much like the same kink—"

"We hope we're wrong," said Dr. Jim. "But think hard. Did you do some trade? Say, maybe in the last two or three months?"

"Well, yeah, I guess I did." Bruce remembered the man's words. "I got a dick that will change your life."

"We hope we're wrong," said Professor Tom. "But it looks like a kink I have found on the X chromosomes of only one type of man. See, the kink isn't on your old chromograph. And see, it's not on Alan's."

"Yes, go on," Alan said.

"We've found it only on the chromosomes of straight men, Kinsey zeros. So far. It doesn't necessarily mean anything. There could be lots of other explanations."

Alan thought about what Mona had told him. "You mean—"

"He means he thinks I'm going straight. What bullshit! That's what you mean, isn't it, professor?"

"We think it's one possibility."

"Bullshit!"

"Maybe so," Dr. Jim said. Professor Tom looked a little hurt. "We are dealing with the unknown," Dr. Jim went on. "As scientists we must not jump to conclusions. But we think it's definitely likely to be catching."

"Definitely likely? What's that mean?" asked Bruce.

"It means, until and unless we know more, only safe sex. Okay?"

"Sure. Sure," said Bruce.

Alan thought, *It's not the safe sex I mind, it's the no sex at all.*

Bruce toyed with the thing on his plate. Finally he brought the fork to his mouth. He got it past his lips. He forced himself to chew. He tried to swallow, but his throat began to close up. He felt like he was going to choke. He spit the chewed yellow mass back onto his plate.

"God Bruce! I can't eat this shit! Why can't we ever have steak and potatoes? Why does it always have to be this foo-foo stuff?"

Alan seemed frozen for a moment. Then the shuddering icy finger of terror raced up his spine, snapping him back to reality.

"Bruce, you spit that out on your plate."

"So?"

"So your napkin is perfectly handy. But look. There it is on the table. You haven't even unfolded it in your lap. You just left it there under your silverware."

"So what? Even Miss Manners must have an occasional lapse."

"It's not just an occasional lapse, Bruce. Look at your hand. What's that in your hand?"

"My fork."

"Your *salad* fork, Bruce." Alan was on the verge of tears. "You tried to eat your quiche lorraine with your salad fork."

"Hey, a fork's a fork."

"No, Bruce. You never used the wrong fork before. Don't you see? Can't you tell?"

"Tell what?"

"Like your fingernails."

Bruce dropped his fork on his plate and looked at the back of his hands. He saw. He tried to hide his hands in his lap. "So? My nails are a little dirty."

"No, Bruce. Not a little dirty. Greasy. Your fingernails are greasy. Tell me, your car needed a tune-up. Does it still need a tune-up?"

"No."

"Bruce, where did you take your car for a tune-up?"

"I don't know. What difference does it make?"

"You know. You know what difference it makes. Why doesn't your car need a tune-up anymore?"

"Because I…"

"Yes, Bruce. Go on."

"Because I tuned it up myself. All right? That's what you wanted me to say. I said it. I'm just getting a little more butch as I get older."

"No, Bruce. Not just a little more butch. Like when you scratch your balls."

"What about when I scratch my balls?"

"When you scratch your balls, you don't put your fingers up to your nose and smell them afterward."

"So?"

"So, Bruce, every gay man in the world smells his fingers after he scratches his balls. Butch numbers do it most of all. You're not getting butcher. You're... you're going..."

"Yes?"

"You're not getting butcher. You're going straight."

Bruce jumped up and overturned the dining table. *"No! No!* You're just jealous. You're jealous because you're just a mincing little fairy who wished she could pass for butch. Get out! Get out of my apartment!"

Alan was appalled. The Picasso sketches were gone. In their place were three paintings on black velvet: one of Elvis; one of wild horses; one of a leering devil offering a cocktail glass, a pair of dice, and a curvaceous blonde. Alan could see only the back of the recliner. The recliner faced the television, which was tuned to a football game. On the mantel, in place of the art deco clock, was a tiny black-and-white TV, tuned to a different football game. The room was littered with beer cans. A wave of dread passed over Alan. His voice cracked as he said, "Bruce? Bruce are you here? I came as soon as I played back your message on the answering machine."

QSFx2

A deafening belch came from the recliner.

"Yes, Alan. Come in. I didn't want you to see me this way. Now I think you better. You were right. I am changing. I am changing into...into Straight-Bruce."

"Oh, no, Bruce!"

"You were right. I've stopped denying it. Pull up the chase lounge."

"You mean the *chaise longue?*"

"Straight-Bruce calls it a chase lounge. Just a second, the game's almost over."

Alan moved the *Road & Track* and the *Hustler* off the chaise longue and pulled it next to Bruce's recliner. Only after he was seated did he dare to look at Bruce. Bruce had changed. The stubble on his face had grown much past the fashionable three days' growth, yet it was not a beard. Bruce was wearing a stained and greasy white T-shirt. The beer belly was now very evident, completely obscuring Bruce's gym-built abs. Then there were the orange-and-blue-plaid Bermuda shorts.

Bruce lifted a leg and farted.

"Wanna brew?" Bruce's hand plunged into the icy water in the Playmate cooler by his recliner.

"Do you have any white wine?" Alan asked, noticing on Bruce's forearm the fresh carbon tattoo of a dripping dagger.

"Naw. Not unless there's some you left here. Come on, goddamn, let's have that instant replay! God did you see that call! It *wasn't* fucking interference, he was going for the ball. Come on, show the goddamn replay! Well, you want a beer or not?"

"You don't have any light?"

"Jesus! Of course I don't have any light. Can't you

166

see? You noticed it first. Can't you see what's happening to me?"

"Yes, Bruce. I can see. Bruce, how are you living? I mean, what are you doing for a living?"

"Oh. You know that after you moved out, they fired me from the salon."

"Yes, I know. What else could they do?"

"Nothing I suppose. Well, they could have found something for me. Maintenance, janitor, something. It's okay. I found a job at an auto-parts store. It's a great bunch of guys. Only..."

"Only?"

"Well, it's only that you and I were buddies for so long—"

"We weren't buddies. We were lovers. Lovers for seven years."

"Five...four...three...two...one! That's the game. Goddamn Wildcats. Goddamn. Dropped a hundred bucks on them last week, too. What was I saying?"

"We were lovers for seven years."

"Oh, yeah. We were buddies for so long. Well, you know, in my situation, old pals are hard to come by. Look, I got some stag flicks at the video store. Let me put one in the machine." Bruce staggered a little as he got up and went to the VCR. He pulled a tape from the stack and slipped it into the machine. Then he threw himself into the recliner. He picked up the remote control.

After the FBI WARNING came the title: *Sorority Snatch*.

"This one's pretty hot," Bruce said as he began to squeeze the lump in his Bermuda shorts.

The opening shot was exterior, at night. A man in

dark clothes crawling into the bushes outside a building. Then, through the blinds, a well-lit room, college pennants on the wall, a teddy bear on the bed. A woman, possibly younger than forty, entered the room. She pulled a collegiate sweater off over her head. She bent, and reaching behind her back, began to unfasten her bra. Reverse angle of the man's eyes through the blinds, sweat forming on his brow, and the muscle of his neck showing that somewhere below, out of view, his hand was moving frantically. Back to the woman. Alan had to look away from the screen.

Bruce had unzipped his Bermuda shorts and was pulling at his long, hooded cock. He noticed Alan looking at him.

"Hey, come on. Look at the flick."

"I can't stand it."

"Yeah, I know. Just don't be so obvious looking at my dick until I get going good. But, you know, we can still get off together, like this. I mean I'm real drunk."

The sight of Bruce's cock getting hard overcame the repulsion Alan felt. Alan unzipped his own trousers slowly.

"Hey," Bruce said. "This wouldn't happen if I wasn't real drunk. But we've been buddies for a long time."

"Lovers, Bruce. We were lovers."

"Straight-Bruce has to call it 'buddies.' Hey, don't stare. Look at my dick out of the corner of your eye if you have to. But pretend you're watching the flick. So you know, we were buddies for a long time. And I had a lot of respect for you."

"You loved me."

"Had a lot of respect for you. And now I...well, you know we had some good times together, and I...I..."

"You're lonely and you miss me."

"Let's just say everybody needs friends. Hey, I love my girlfriend. But she's pregnant now, you know. Oh, I guess you didn't know." Bruce spit on his hand and stroked the length of his cock.

Alan's own cock was hard now. He couldn't help himself. He watched Bruce's cock out of the corner of his eye. He tried to block out the picture of the woman on the TV screen. He began stroking his own cock.

"Anyway, so I watch the videos for the time being."

"Because you're afraid that if you fuck your girlfriend, you'll dent the baby's little head. Straight men always think that."

"They do? Well, it does seem to me that my cock is even bigger than it was. I measured it and it's not. But my cock just seems huge now. I guess that's part of getting to be Straight-Bruce. Anyway, I'm real drunk, or this wouldn't be happening. I'm real drunk and horny. So, look, why don't you just suck my dick a little while I watch the video."

"Bruce!"

"Come on, Alan. You've done it before. I don't get much head these days."

"Bruce, you know the doctor said it was catching."

"He wasn't sure. And they don't know everything. You know you want it. C'mon. Please. I may not be this drunk again."

Alan stopped pulling on his cock. His erection was beginning to wilt. "I get it now. You want me to catch it. You want me to be just like you."

"It won't be so bad. C'mon. You'd love to have my dick again. Look, my girlfriend has a sister. It won't really be so bad. Like we can go fishing together. I'll show you how to work on cars. Maybe when the girls go to see their mother, maybe we could get drunk together, maybe real drunk. Maybe things would be like old times."

Alan's eyes widened with horror. "No! It wouldn't be like old times... You...you want me to be just like you!"

Bruce hadn't stopped jerking on his cock. When the tip poked out of the foreskin, it was very red. A pearl of precome formed at his cockslit. He peeled the foreskin all the way back.

"Ick! God, Bruce! It's—it's smegma! You haven't been washing!"

"Headcheese. Gives it flavor. You'll love it."

"No, Bruce, no!"

"Enough arguing. Suck my dick, faggot!" Bruce's hand caught the back of Alan's neck.

"No, Bruce! No! How can you do this to me?"

"Yes, yes. C'mon. Join me. I need a buddy. C'mon, I'm about to get it. Drink my cum. Swallow my straight cum, cocksucker!" Bruce drew Alan's head closer. Alan's eyes glazed over with fear. "We'll be together this way, Alan. We'll be buddies. C'mon, take my wad."

Alan tried to pull back, but he could not take his eyes off the cock, Bruce's huge, hot, throbbing cock. He couldn't look away. Bruce's hand pulled Alan's neck.

"No, Bruce, please don't make me!" Tears began forming in Alan's eyes.

"I'm so lonely. Take it, take it, and then we'll be friends. You'll be my brother-in-law. C'mon, hurry.

Don't you know how hard it is for Straight-Bruce to have friends? Eat me, faggot, eat me!" Bruce's balls clamped up close to the base of his cock.

Alan couldn't pull away. His lover was still somewhere inside of Straight-Bruce. He couldn't help himself. He opened his mouth. Bruce's cock aimed at his mouth, coming closer and closer. Bruce's balls began to jump.

"How long has this been going on!" Mona shrieked as he stood at the open door in full drag.

Alan looked up.

"Oh, no!" Bruce's cock pumped out its wad, four, five spurts arcing into the air and splatting against the TV screen.

"Nobody answered me when I knocked," Mona explained. "So I didn't think anyone would mind if I let myself in."

"Oh, God, it's wasted! You wasted my wad, you little cocksucker."

"Help! Mona, get me out of here!"

"Run, Alan, run! The Volvo's downstairs. I left the motor running."

Alan broke free and ran toward Mona and the door.

"No. Come back. Come back. I can get it up again. It will only take a second. Oh, gee, if only I weren't so drunk." Bruce staggered to his feet, pulling frantically at his limp cock.

"Ta-ta, Bruce!" Mona waved. "Sorry we have to run. I guess you're so drunk that you won't remember this in the morning, will you?"

As the Volvo pulled away from the curb, Alan noticed that his trousers were still unzipped. He zipped them.

"Thank goodness you came by when you did, Mona. He was about to...about to..."

"There, there. I know. The professor is one of my afternoon callers. He told me all about it. You just have to stay away from here for a few more weeks. Bruce has bought a house in the suburbs. By the time he moves, we think the transformation will be complete."

"You mean…"

"Yes. He'll be a Kinsey zero. He won't even want to try something like that again."

Caught in the Volvo, a fly buzzed past Alan's cheek. Alan began to sob softly.

The Masquerade Erotic Newsletter

◆◆◆◆◆◆◆◆◆◆◆◆◆◆◆◆◆◆◆◆◆◆◆

FICTION, ESSAYS, REVIEWS, PHOTOGRAPHY, INTERVIEWS, EXPOSÉS, AND MUCH MORE!

"One of my favorite sex zines featuring some of the best articles on erotica fetishes, sex clubs and the politics of porn." —*Factsheet Five*

"I recommend a subscription to *The Masquerade Erotic Newsletter*.... They feature short articles on "the scene"...an occasional fiction piece, and reviews of other erotic literature. Recent issues have featured intelligent prose by the likes of Trish Thomas, David Aaron Clark, Pat Califia, Laura Antoniou, Lily Burana, John Preston, and others.... it's good stuff." —*Black Sheets*

"A classy, bi-monthly magazine..." —*Betty Paginated*

"It's always a treat to see a copy of *The Masquerade Erotic Newsletter*, for it brings a sophisticated and unexpected point of view to bear on the world of erotica, and does this with intelligence, tolerance, and compassion." —Martin Shepard, co-publisher, The Permanent Press

"Publishes great articles, interviews and pix which in many cases are truly erotic and which deal non-judgementally with the full array of human sexuality, a far cry from much of the material which passes itself off under that title.... *Masquerade Erotic Newsletter* is fucking great." —*Eddie, the Magazine*

"We always enjoy receiving your *Masquerade Newsletter* and seeing the variety of subjects covered...." —*body art*

"*Masquerade Erotic Newsletter* is probably the best newsletter I have ever seen." —*Secret International*

"The latest issue is absolutely lovely. Marvelous images...." —*The Boudoir Noir*

"I must say that the *Newsletter* is fabulous...."
—Tuppy Owens, Publisher, Author, Sex Therapist

"Fascinating articles on all aspects of sex..." —*Desire*

◆◆◆◆◆◆◆◆◆◆◆◆◆◆◆◆◆◆◆◆◆◆◆

The Masquerade Erotic Newsletter

"Here's a very provocative, very professional [newsletter]...made up of intelligent erotic writing... Stimulating, yet not sleazy photos add to the picture and also help make this zine a high quality publication." —Gray Areas

From **Masquerade Books**, the World's Leading Publisher of Erotica, comes *The Masquerade Erotic Newsletter*—the best source for provocative, cutting-edge fiction, sizzling pictorials, scintillating and illuminating exposes of the sex industry, and probing reviews of the latest books and videos.

Featured writers and articles have included:

Lars Eighner • *Why I Write Gay Erotica*
Pat Califia • *Among Us, Against Us*
Felice Picano • *An Interview with Samuel R. Delany*
Samuel R. Delany • *The Mad Man* (excerpt)
Maxim Jakubowski • *Essex House: The Rise and Fall of Speculative Erotica*
Red Jordan Arobateau • *Reflections of a Lesbian Trick*
Aaron Travis • *Lust*
Nancy Ava Miller, M. Ed. • *Beyond Personal*
Tuppy Owens • *Female Erotica in Great Britain*
Trish Thomas • *From Dyke to Dude*
Barbara Nitke • *Resurrection*
and many more....

The newsletter has also featured stunning photo essays by such masters of fetish photography as **Robert Chouraqui**, **Eric Kroll**, **Richard Kern**, and **Trevor Watson**.

A one-year subscription (6 issues) to the *Newsletter* costs $30.00. Use the accompanying coupon to subscribe now—for an uninterrupted string of the most provocative of pleasures (as well as a special gift, offered to subscribers only!).

Free GIFT

WHEN YOU SUBSCRIBE TO:
The Masquerade Erotic Newsletter

Receive two **MASQUERADE** books of your choice.

Please send me Two MASQUERADE Books Free!

1. _____

2. _____

☐ I've enclosed my payment of $30.00 for a one-year subscription (six issues) to: *THE MASQUERADE EROTIC NEWSLETTER.*

Name _____

Address _____

City _____ State _____ Zip _____

Tel. (____) _____

Payment ☐ Check ☐ Money Order ☐ Visa ☐ MC.

Card No. _____

Exp. Date _____

Please allow 4–6 weeks delivery. No C.O.D. orders. Please make all checks payable to Masquerade Books, 801 Second Avenue, N.Y., N.Y., 10017. Payable in U.S. currency only. Order by phone: 1-800-375-2356 or fax, 212 986-7355   **X74L**

THE ARENA

$4.95 (CANADA $5.95) • BADBOY

JOHN PRESTON

BADBOY

JOHN PRESTON

Tales from the Dark Lord II $4.95/176-4
The second volume of acclaimed eroticist John Preston's masterful short stories. Also includes an interview with the author, and an explicit screenplay written for pornstar Scott O'Hara. An explosive collection from one of erotic publishing's most fertile imaginations.

Tales from the Dark Lord $5.95/323-6
A new collection of twelve stunning works from the man *Lambda Book Report* called "the Dark Lord of gay erotica." The relentless ritual of lust and surrender is explored in all its manifestations in this heart-stopping triumph of authority and vision from the Dark Lord!

The Arena $4.95/3083-0
There is a place on the edge of fantasy where every desire is indulged with abandon. Men go there to unleash beasts, to let demons roam free, to abolish all limits. At the center of each tale are the men who serve there, who offer themselves for the consummation of any passion, whose own bottomless urges compel their endless subservience.

The Heir • The King $4.95/3048-2
The ground-breaking novel *The Heir*, written in the lyric voice of the ancient myths, tells the story of a world where slaves and masters create a new sexual society. This edition also includes a completely original work, *The King*, the story of a soldier who discovers his monarch's most secret desires. Available only from Badboy.

Mr. Benson $4.95/3041-5
A classic erotic novel from a time when there was no limit to what a man could dream of doing.... Jamie is an aimless young man lucky enough to encounter Mr. Benson. He is soon led down the path of erotic enlightenment, learning to accept cruelty as love, anguish as affection, and this man as his master. From an opulent penthouse to the infamous Mineshaft, Jamie's incredible adventures never fail to excite—especially when the going gets rough! First serialized in *Drummer*, *Mr. Benson* became an immediate classic that inspired many imitators. Preston's knockout novel returns to claim the territory it mapped out years ago. The first runaway success in gay SM literature, *Mr. Benson* is sure to inspire further generations.

THE MISSION OF ALEX KANE

Sweet Dreams $4.95/3062-8
It's the triumphant return of gay action hero Alex Kane! This classic series has been revised and updated especially for Badboy, and includes loads of raw action. In *Sweet Dreams*, Alex travels to Boston where he takes on a street gang that stalks gay teenagers. Mighty Alex Kane wreaks a fierce and terrible vengeance on those who prey on gay people everywhere!

Golden Years $4.95/3069-5
When evil threatens the plans of a group of older gay men, Kane's got the muscle to take it head on. Along the way, he wins the support—and very specialized attentions—of a cowboy plucked right out of the Old West. But Kane and the Cowboy have a surprise waiting for them....

Deadly Lies $4.95/3076-8
Politics is a dirty business and the dirt becomes deadly when a political smear campaign targets gay men. Who better to clean things up than Alex Kane! Alex comes to protect the dreams, and lives, of gay men imperiled by lies.

Stolen Moments $4.95/3098-9
Houston's evolving gay community is victimized by a malicious newspaper editor who is more than willing to sacrifice gays on the altar of circulation. He never counted on Alex Kane, fearless defender of gay dreams and desires everywhere.

Secret Danger $4.95/111-X
Homophobia: a pernicious social ill hardly confined by America's borders. Alex Kane and the faithful Danny are called to a small European country, where a group of gay tourists is being held hostage by ruthless terrorists. Luckily, the Mission of Alex Kane stands as firm foreign policy.

Lethal Silence $4.95/125-X
The Mission of Alex Kane thunders to a conclusion. Chicago becomes the scene of the right-wing's most noxious plan—facilitated by unholy political alliances. Alex and Danny head to the Windy City to take up battle with the mercenaries who would squash gay men underfoot.

JAY SHAFFER

Shooters $5.95/284-1
A new set of stories from the author of the best-selling erotic collections *Wet Dreams, Full Service* and *Animal Handlers*. No mere catalog of random acts, *Shooters* tells the stories of a variety of stunning men and the ways they connect in sexual and non-sexual ways. A virtuoso storyteller, Shaffer always gets his man.

Animal Handlers $4.95/264-7
Another volume from a master of scorching fiction. In Shaffer's world, each and every man finally succumbs to the animal urges deep inside. And if there's any creature that promises a wild time, it's a beast who's been caged for far too long.

Full Service $4.95/150-0
A baker's dirty dozen from the author of *Wet Dreams*. Wild men build up steam until they finally let loose. No-nonsense guys bear down hard on each other as they work their way toward release in this finely detailed assortment of masculine fantasies.

Wet Dreams $4.95/142-X
These tales take a hot look at the obsessions that keep men up all night—from simple skin-on-skin to more unusual pleasures. Provocative and affecting, this is a nightful of dreams you won't forget in the morning.

D.V. SADERO

Revolt of the Naked $4.95/261-2
In a distant galaxy, there are two classes of humans: Freemen and Nakeds. Freemen are full citizens in this system, which allows for the buying and selling of Nakeds at whim. Nakeds live only to serve their Masters, and obey every sexual order with haste and devotion. Until the day of revolution—when an army of sex toys rises in anger....

In the Alley $4.95/144-6
Twenty cut-to-the-chase yarns inspired by the all-American male. Hardworking men—from cops to carpenters—bring their own special skills and impressive tools to the most satisfying job of all: capturing and breaking the male sexual beast. Hot, incisive and way over the top!

Wet Dreams

Jay Shaffer

$4.95 • BADBOY

KYLE STONE

Hot Bauds $5.95/285-X
The author of *Fantasy Board* and *The Initiation of PB 500* combed cyberspace for the hottest fantasies of the world's horniest hackers. From bulletin boards called Studs, The Mine Shaft, Back Door and the like, Stone has assembled the first collection of the raunchy erotica so many gay men cruise the Information Superhighway for. Plug in—and get ready to download....

Fantasy Board $4.95/212-4
The author of the scalding sci-fi adventures of PB 500 explores the more foreseeable future—through the intertwined lives (and private parts) of a collection of randy computer hackers. On the Lambda Gate BBS, every hot and horny male is in search of a little virtual satisfaction.contented.

The Citadel $4.95/198-5
The thundering sequel to *The Initiation of PB 500*. Having proven himself worthy of his stunning master, Micah—now known only as '500'—will face new challenges and hardships after his entry into the forbidding Citadel. Only his master knows what awaits—and whether Micah will again distinguish himself as the perfect instrument of pleasure....

Rituals $4.95/168-3
Via a computer bulletin board, a young man finds himself drawn into a series of sexual rites that transform him into the willing slave of a mysterious stranger. Gradually, all vestiges of his former life are thrown off, and he learns to live for his Master's touch.... A high-tech fable of sexual surrender.

The Initiation PB 500 $4.95/141-1
He is a stranger on their planet, unschooled in their language, and ignorant of their customs. But this man, Micah—now known only by his number—will soon be trained in every last detail of erotic personal service. And, once nurtured and transformed into the perfect physical specimen, he must begin proving himself worthy of the master who has chosen him.... A scalding sci-fi epic, continued in *The Citadel*.

PHIL ANDROS

The Joy Spot $5.95/301-5
"Andros gives to the gay mind what Tom of Finland gives the gay eye—this is archetypal stuff. There's none better."
—John F. Karr, *Manifest Reader*

A classic from one of the founding fathers of gay porn. *The Joy Spot* looks at some of Andros' favorite types—cops, servicemen, truck drivers—and the sleaze they love. Nothing's too rough, and these men are always ready. So get ready to give it up—or have it taken by force!

ROBERT BAHR

Sex Show $4.95/225-6
Luscious dancing boys. Brazen, explicit acts. Unending stimulation. Take a seat, and get very comfortable, because the curtain's going up on a show no discriminating appetite can afford to miss. And the award for Best Performer...is up to you....

"BIG" BILL JACKSON

Eighth Wonder $4.95/200-0
"Big" Bill Jackson's always the randiest guy in town—no matter what town he's in. From the bright lights and back rooms of New York to the open fields and sweaty bods of a small Southern town, "Big" Bill always manages to cause a scene, and the more actors he can involve, the better! Like the man's name says, he's got more than enough for everyone, and turns nobody down....

1 900 745-HUNG

THE connection for hot handsfull of eager guys! No credit card needed—so call now for access to the hottest party line available. Spill it all to bad boys from across the country! (Must be over 18.) Pick one up now.... $3.98 per minute.

JASON FURY

The Rope Above, the Bed Below $4.95/269-8

The irresistible Jason Fury returns—and if you thought his earlier adventures were hot, this volume will blow you away! Once again, our built, blond hero finds himself in the oddest—and most compromising—positions imaginable.

Eric's Body $4.95/151-9

Meet Jason Fury—blond, blue-eyed and up for anything. Perennial favorites in the gay press, Fury's sexiest tales are collected in book form for the first time. Ranging from the bittersweet to the surreal, these stories follow the irresistible Jason through sexual adventures unlike any you have ever read....

JOHN ROWBERRY

Lewd Conduct $4.95/3091-1

Flesh-and-blood men vie for power, pleasure and surrender in each of these feverish stories, and no one walks away from his steamy encounter unsated. Rowberry's men are unafraid to push the limits of civilized behavior in search of the elusive and empowering conquest.

LARS EIGHNER

Whispered in the Dark $5.95/286-8

Lars Eighner continues to produce gay fiction whose quality rivals the best in the genre. *Whispered in the Dark* continues to demonstrate Eighner's unique combination of strengths: poetic descriptive power, an unfailing ear for dialogue, and a finely tuned feeling for the nuances of male passion. *Whispered in the Dark* reasserts Eighner's claim to mastery of the gay erotica genre.

American Prelude $4.95/170-5

Another volume of irresistible Eighner tales. Praised by *The New York Times*, Eighner is widely recognized as one of our best, most exciting gay writers. What the *Times* won't admit, however, is that he is also one of gay erotica's true masters—and *American Prelude* shows why.

Bayou Boy $4.95/3084-9

Another collection of well-tuned stories from one of our finest writers. Witty and incisive, each tale explores the many ways men work up a sweat in the steamy Southwest. *Bayou Boy* also includes the "Houston Streets" stories—sexy, touching tales of growing up gay in a fast-changing world. Street smart and razor sharp—and guaranteed to warm the coldest night!

B.M.O.C. $4.95/3077-6

In a college town known as "the Athens of the Southwest," studs of every stripe are up all night—studying, naturally. In *B.M.O.C.*, Lars Eighner includes the very best of his short stories, sure to appeal to the collegian in every man. Relive university life the way it was *supposed* to be, with a cast of handsome honor students majoring in Human Homosexuality.

CALDWELL/EIGHNER

QSFx2 $5.95/278-7

One volume of the wickedest, wildest, other-worldliest yarns from two master storytellers—Clay Caldwell and Lars Eighner, the highly-acclaimed author of *Travels With Lizbeth*. Both eroticists take a trip to the furthest reaches of the sexual imagination, sending back ten stories proving that as much as things change, one thing will always remain the same....

AARON TRAVIS

In the Blood $5.95/283-3
Written when Travis had just begun to explore the true power of the erotic imagination, these stories laid the groundwork for later masterpieces. Among the many rewarding rarities included in this volume: "In the Blood"—a heart-pounding descent into sexual vampirism, written with the furious erotic power that has distinguished Travis' work from the beginning.

The Flesh Fables $4.95/243-4
One of Travis' best collections, finally rereleased. *The Flesh Fables* includes "Blue Light," his most famous story, as well as other masterpieces that established him as the erotic writer to watch. And watch carefully, because Travis always buries a surprise somewhere beneath his scorching detail....

Slaves of the Empire $4.95/3054-7
The return of an undisputed classic from this master of the erotic genre.
"*Slaves of the Empire* is a wonderful mythic tale. Set against the backdrop of the exotic and powerful Roman Empire, this wonderfully written novel explores the timeless questions of light and dark in male sexuality. Travis has shown himself expert in manipulating the most primal themes and images. The locale may be the ancient world, but these are the slaves and masters of our time...."
—John Preston

Big Shots $4.95/112-8
Two fierce tales in one electrifying volume. In *Beirut*, Travis tells the story of ultimate military power and erotic subjugation; *Kip*, Travis' hypersexed and sinister take on *film noir*, appears in unexpurgated form for the first time—including the final, overwhelming chapter. Unforgettable acts and relentless passions dominate these chronicles of unimaginable lust—as seen from the points of view of raging, powerful men, and the bottomless submissives who yield to their desires. One of our rawest, most unrelenting titles.

Exposed $4.95/126-8
A volume of shorter Travis tales, each providing a unique glimpse of the horny gay male in his natural environment! Cops, college jocks, ancient Romans—even Sherlock Holmes and his loyal Watson—cruise these pages, fresh from the throbbing pen of one of our hottest authors.

Beast of Burden $4.95/105-5
Five ferocious tales from a master of lascivious prose. Innocents surrender to the brutal sexual mastery of their superiors, as taboos are shattered and replaced with the unwritten rules of masculine conquest. Intense, extreme—and totally Travis.

CLAY CALDWELL

Service, Stud $5.95/336-8
From the author of the sexy sci-fi epic *All-Stud*, comes another look at the gay future. The setting is the Los Angeles of a distant future. Here the all-male populace is divided between the served and the servants—an arrangement guaranteeing the erotic satisfaction of all involved. Until, of course, one pugnacious young stud challenges authority, and the sexual rules it so rigidly enforces....

Stud Shorts $5.95/320-1
"If anything, Caldwell's charm is more powerful, his nostalgia more poignant, the horniness he captures more sweetly, achingly acute than ever."
—Aaron Travis
A new collection of this legendary writer's latest sex-fiction. With his customary candor, Caldwell tells all about cops, cadets, truckers, farmboys (and many more) in these dirty jewels.

Tailpipe Trucker $5.95/296-5
With *Tailpipe Trucker*, Clay Caldwell set the cornerstone of "trucker porn"—a story revolving around the age-old fantasy of horny men on the road. In prose as free and unvarnished as a cross-country highway, Caldwell tells the truth about Trag and Curly—two men hot for the feeling of sweaty manflesh.

Queers Like Us $4.95/262-0
"This is Caldwell at his most charming."
—Aaron Travis
For years the name Clay Caldwell has been synonymous with the hottest, most finely crafted gay tales available. *Queers Like Us* is one of his best: the story of a randy mailman's trek through a landscape of willing, available studs.

All-Stud $4.95/104-7
An incredible, erotic trip into the gay future. This classic, sex-soaked tale takes place under the watchful eye of Number Ten: an omniscient figure who has decreed unabashed promiscuity as the law of his all-male land. Men exist to serve men, and all surrender to state-sanctioned fleshly indulgence.

HODDY ALLEN

Al $5.95/302-3
Al is a remarkable young man. With his long brown hair, bright green eyes and eagerness to please, many would consider him the perfect submissive. Many would like to mark him as their own—but it is at that point that Al stops. One day Al relates the entire astounding tale of his life....

1 800 906-HUNK

Hardcore phone action for *real* men. A scorching assembly of studs is waiting for your call—and eager to give you the head-trip of your life! Totally live, guaranteed one-on-one encounters. (Must be over 18.) No credit card needed. $3.98 per minute.

KEY LINCOLN

Submission Holds $4.95/266-3
A bright young talent unleashes his first collection of gay erotica. From tough to tender, the men between these covers stop at nothing to get what they want. These sweat-soaked tales show just how bad boys can really get....

TOM BACCHUS

Rahm $5.95/315-5
A volume spanning the many ages of hardcore queer lust—from Creation to the modern day. The imagination of Tom Bacchus brings to life an extraordinary assortment of characters, from the Father of Us All to the cowpoke next door, the early gay literati to rude, queercore mosh rats. No one is better than Bacchus at staking out sexual territory with a swagger and a sly grin.

Bone $4.95/177-2
Queer musings from the pen of one of today's hottest young talents. A fresh outlook on fleshly indulgence yields more than a few pleasant surprises. Horny Tom Bacchus maps out the tricking ground of a new generation.

VINCE GILMAN

The Slave Prince $4.95/199-3
"...*I was never a slave, Pasha thought, smiling proudly to himself. I used to hold orgies with the men from my father's honor guard, late at night, when my father was busy with his harem boys and knew no better....*"
A runaway royal learns the true meaning of power when he comes under the hand of Korat—a man well-versed in the many ways of subjugating a young man to his relentless sexual appetite.

2069 TRILOGY

LARRY TOWNSEND

BOB VICKERY

Skin Deep $4.95/265-5
Talk about "something for everyone!" *Skin Deep* contains so many varied beauties no one will go away unsatisfied. No tantalizing morsel of manflesh is overlooked—or left unexplored! Beauty may be only skin deep, but a handful of beautiful skin is a tempting proposition.

JAMES MEDLEY

Huck and Billy $4.95/245-0
Young love is always the sweetest, always the most sorrowful. Young lust, on the other hand, knows no bounds—and is often the hottest of one's life! Huck and Billy explore the desires that course through their young male bodies, determined to plumb the lusty depths of passion. Sweet and hot. Very hot.

LARRY TOWNSEND

Beware the God Who Smiles $5.95/321-X
A torrid time-travel tale from one of gay erotica's most notorious writers. Two lusty young Americans are transported to ancient Egypt—where they are embroiled in regional warfare and taken as slaves by marauding barbarians. The key to escape from this brutal bondage lies in their own rampant libidos, and urges as old as time itself.

The Construction Worker $5.95/298-1
A young, hung construction worker is sent to a building project in Central America, where he is shocked to find some ancient and unusual traditions in practice. In this isolated location, man-to-man sex is the accepted norm. The young stud quickly fits right in (and quite snugly)—until he senses that beneath the constant sexual shenanigans there moves an almost supernatural force. Soon, nothing is what it seems....

2069 Trilogy (This one-volume collection only **$6.95**) 244-2
For the first time, Larry Townsend's early science-fiction trilogy appears in one volume! Set in a future world, the *2069 Trilogy* includes the tight plotting and shameless male pleasure that established him as one of gay erotica's first masters. This special one-volume edition available only from Badboy.

Mind Master $4.95/209-4
Who better to explore the territory of erotic dominance and submission than an author who helped define the genre—and knows that ultimate mastery always transcends the physical.

The Long Leather Cord $4.95/201-9
Chuck's stepfather is an enigma: never lacking in money or clandestine male visitors with whom he enacts intense sexual rituals. As Chuck comes to terms with his own savage desires, he begins to unravel his stepfather's mystery.

Man Sword $4.95/188-8
The *tres gai* tale of France's King Henri III. Unimaginably spoiled by his mother—the infamous Catherine de Medici—Henri is groomed from a young age to assume the throne of France. Along the way, he encounters enough sexual schemers and randy politicos to alter one's picture of history forever!

The Faustus Contract $4.95/167-5
Two attractive young men desperately need $1000. Will do anything. Travel OK. Danger OK. Call anytime... Two cocky young hustlers get more than they bargained for in this story of lust and its discontents.

The Gay Adventures of Captain Goose $4.95/169-1
The hot and tender young Jerome Gander is sentenced to serve aboard the *H.M.S. Faerigold*—a ship manned by the most hardened, unrepentant criminals. In no time, Gander becomes well-versed in the ways of men at sea, and the *Faerigold* becomes the most notorious ship of its day.

Chains $4.95/158-6
Picking up street punks has always been risky, but in Larry Townsend's classic *Chains*, it sets off a string of events that must be read to be believed. One of Townsend's most remarkable works, *Chains* explores the dynamics of the male sexual bond—and what happens when a weak link finally gives....

Kiss of Leather $4.95/161-6
Acclaimed gay porn pioneer Larry Townsend's first leather title. A look at the acts and attitudes of an earlier generation of leathermen, *Kiss of Leather* is full to bursting with the gritty, raw action that has distinguished Townsend's work for years. Pain and pleasure mix in this tightly-plotted tale.

Run No More $4.95/152-7
The continuation of Larry Townsend's legendary *Run, Little Leather Boy*. This volume follows the further adventures of Townsend's leatherclad narrator as he travels every sexual byway available to the S/M male. As he works his way toward elite circles, Wayne begins to make shocking discoveries....

Run, Little Leather Boy $4.95/143-8
The classic story of one young man's sexual awakening. A chronic underachiever, Wayne seems to be going nowhere fast. When his father puts him to work for a living, Wayne soon finds himself bored with the everyday—and increasingly drawn to the masculine intensity of a dark sexual underground....

The Scorpius Equation $4.95/119-5
A sex-packed science fiction adventure from the fertile imagination of Larry Townsend. Set in the far future, *The Scorpius Equation* is the story of a man caught between the demands of two galactic empires. Our randy hero must match wits—and more—with the incredible forces that rule his world.

The Sexual Adventures of Sherlock Holmes $4.95/3097-0
Holmes' most satisfying adventures, from the unexpurgated memoirs of the faithful Mr. Watson. "A Study in Scarlet" is transformed to expose Mrs. Hudson as a man in drag, the Diogenes Club as an S/M arena, and clues only Sherlock Holmes could piece together. A baffling tale of sex and mystery.

DEREK ADAMS

My Double Life $5.95/314-7
Every man leads a double life, dividing his hours between the mundanities of the day and the outrageous pursuits of the night. In this, his second collection of stories, the author of *Boy Toy* and creator of sexy P.I. Miles Diamond shines a little light on what men do when no one's looking. Derek Adams proves, once again, that he's the ultimate chronicler of our wicked ways.

Boy Toy $4.95/260-4
Poor Brendan Callan—sent to the Brentwood Academy against his will, he soon finds himself the guinea pig of a crazed geneticist. Brendan becomes irresistibly alluring—a talent designed for endless pleasure, but coveted by others for the most unsavory means....

Heat Wave $4.95/159-4
"His body was draped in baggy clothes, but there was hardly any doubt that they covered anything less than perfection.... His slacks were cinched tight around a narrow waist, and the rise of flesh pushing against the thin fabric promised a firm, melon-shaped ass....The little flame of lust that had been tickling in my belly flared into a full-scale conflagration..."

Miles Diamond and the Demon of Death $4.95/251-5
Derek Adams' gay gumshoe Miles Diamond returns for further adventures of the good old-fashioned private eye variety. Miles always seems to find himself in the stickiest situations—with any stud whose path he crosses! His adventures with "The Demon of Death" promise another carnal carnival.

The Adventures of Miles Diamond $4.95/118-7
The hot adventures of horny P.I. Miles Diamond. "The Case of the Missing Twin" promises to be a most rewarding case, packed as it is with randy studs. Miles sets about uncovering all as he tracks down the elusive and delectable Daniel Travis.... The volume that made Miles Diamond a sensation.

KELVIN BELIELE

If the Shoe Fits $4.95/223-X
An essential and winning volume of tales exploring a world where randy boys can't help but do what comes naturally—as often as possible! Sweaty male bodies grapple in pleasure, proving the old adage: if the shoe fits, one might as well slip right in....

VICTOR TERRY

WHiPs $4.95/254-X
Connoisseurs of gay writing have known Victor Terry's work for some time. With *WHiPs*, Terry joins BADBOY's roster at last with this punishing collection of short stories. Cruising for a hot man? You'd better be, because one way or another, these WHiPs—officers of the Wyoming Highway Patrol—are gonna pull you over for a little impromptu interrogation....

MAX EXANDER

Deeds of the Night: Tales of Eros and Passion $5.95/348-1
MAXimum porn! Exander's a writer who's seen it all—and is more than happy to describe every inch of it in pulsating detail. From the man behind *Mansex* and *Leathersex*—two whirlwind tours of the hypermasculine libido—comes another unrestrained volume of sweat-soaked fantasies.

Leathersex $4.95/210-8
Another volume of hard-hitting tales from merciless Max Exander. This time he focuses on the leatherclad lust that draws together only the most willing and talented of tops and bottoms—for an all-out orgy of limitless surrender and control....

Mansex $4.95/160-8
"Tex was all his name implied: tall, lanky but muscular, with reddish-blond hair and a handsome, chiseled face that was somewhat leathered. Mark was the classic leatherman: a huge, dark stud in chaps, with a big black moustache, hairy chest and enormous muscles. Exactly the kind of men Todd liked—strong, hunky, masculine, ready to take control...." Rough sex for rugged men.

TOM CAFFREY

Hitting Home $4.95/222-1
One of our newest Badboys weighs in with a scorching collection of stories. Titillating and compelling, the stories in *Hitting Home* make a strong case for there being only one thing on a man's mind.

TORSTEN BARRING

Prisoners of Torquemada $5.95/252-3
The infamously unsparing Torsten Barring (*The Switch*, *Peter Thornwell*, *Shadowman*) weighs in with another volume sure to push you over the edge. How cruel is the "therapy" practiced at Casa Torquemada? Rest assured that Barring is just the writer to evoke such steamy malevolence.

Shadowman $4.95/178-0
From spoiled Southern aristocrats to randy youths sowing wild oats at the local picture show, Barring's imagination works overtime in these vignettes of homolust—past, present and future.

Peter Thornwell $4.95/149-7
Follow the exploits of Peter Thornwell as he goes from misspent youth to scandalous stardom, all thanks to an insatiable libido and love for the lash. Peter and his sex-crazed sidekicks find themselves pursued by merciless men from all walks of life in this torrid take on Horatio Alger.

THE SWITCH

Torsten Barring

The Switch $4.95/3061-X
Sometimes a man needs a good whipping, and *The Switch* certainly makes a case! Laced with images of men "in too-tight Levi's, with the faces of angels... and the bodies of devils." Packed with hot studs and unrelenting passions.

SONNY FORD
Reunion in Florence $4.95/3070-9
Captured by Turks, Adrian and Tristan will do anything to save their heads. When Tristan is threatened by a Sultan's jealousy, Adrian begins his quest for the only man alive who can replace Tristan as the object of the Sultan's lust. The two soon learn to rely on their wild sexual imaginations.

ROGER HARMAN
First Person $4.95/179-9
A highly personal collection. Each story here takes the form of an uncensored confessional—told by men who've got plenty to confess! From the "first time ever" to firsts of different kinds, *First Person* tells truths too hot to be fiction.

CHRISTOPHER MORGAN
Muscle Bound $4.95/3028-8
In the New York City bodybuilding scene, country boy Tommy joins forces with sexy Will Rodriguez in a battle of wits and biceps at the hottest gym in the Village, where the weak are bound and crushed by iron-pumping gods. Muscle-studs run amuck!

SEAN MARTIN
Scrapbook $4.95/224-8
Imagine a book filled with only the best, most vivid remembrances...a book brimming with every hot, sexy encounter its pages can hold... Now you need only open up *Scrapbook* to know that such a volume really exists....

CARO SOLES & STAN TAL
Bizarre Dreams $4.95/187-X
An anthology of stirring voices dedicated to exploring the dark side of human fantasy. Including such BADBOY favorites as John Preston, Lars Eighner and Kyle Stone, *Bizarre Dreams* brings together the most talented practitioners of "dark fantasy": the most forbidden sexual realm of all.

J.A. GUERRA
BADBOY Fantasies $4.95/3049-0
When love eludes them—lust will do! Thrill-seeking men caught up in vivid dreams and dark mysteries—these are the brief encounters you'll pant and gasp over in *Badboy Fantasies*.

Slow Burn $4.95/3042-3
Welcome to the Body Shoppe, where men's lives cross in the pursuit of muscle. Torsos get lean and hard, pecs widen, and stomachs ripple in these sexy stories of the power and perils of physical perfection.

Men at Work $4.95/3027-X
He's the most gorgeous man you have ever seen. You yearn for his touch at night in your empty bed; but he's your co-worker! A collection of eight sizzling stories of man-to-man on-the-job training.

DAVE KINNICK
Sorry I Asked $4.95/3090-3
Unexpurgated interviews with gay porn's rank and file. Dave Kinnick, longtime video reviewer for *Advocate Men*, gets personal with the men behind (and under) the "stars," and reveals the dirt and details of the porn business.

MICHAEL LOWENTHAL, ED.

The BADBOY Erotic Library Volume I $4.95/190-X
A Secret Life, Imre, Sins of the Cities of the Plain, Teleny and *more*—the hottest sections of these perennial favorites come together for the first time.

The BADBOY Erotic Library Volume II $4.95/211-6
This time, selections are taken from *Mike and Me* and *Muscle Bound, Men at Work, Badboy Fantasies,* and *Slowburn.*

ANONYMOUS

A Secret Life $4.95/3017-2
Meet Master Charles: only eighteen, and *quite* innocent, until his arrival at the Sir Percival's Royal Academy, where the daily lessons are supplemented with a crash course in pure, sweet sexual heat!

Sins of the Cities of the Plain $5.95/322-8
Indulge yourself in the scorching memoirs of young man-about-town Jack Saul. From his earliest erotic moments with Jerry in the dark of his bedchamber, to his shocking dalliances with the lords and "ladies" of British high society, Jack's positively *sinful* escapades grow wilder with every chapter!

Imre $4.95/3019-9
What dark secrets, what fiery passions lay hidden behind strikingly beautiful Lieutenant Imre's emerald eyes? An extraordinary lost classic of fantasy, obsession, gay erotic desire, and romance in a tiny town on the eve of WWI.

Teleny $4.95/3020-2
A dark Victorian classic, often attributed to Oscar Wilde. A young stud of independent means seeks only a succession of voluptuous and forbidden pleasures, but instead finds love and tragedy when he becomes embroiled in a mysterious cult devoted to fulfilling only the very darkest of fantasies.

Mike and Me $4.95/3035-0
Mike joined the gym squad to bulk up on muscle. Little did he know he'd be turning on every sexy muscle jock in Minnesota! Hard bodies collide in a series of workouts designed to generate a whole lot more than rips and cuts.

PAT CALIFIA

The Sexpert $4.95/3034-2
For many years now, the sophisticated gay man has known that he can turn to one authority for answers to virtually any question on the subjects of intimacy and sexual performance. Straight from the pages of *Advocate Men* comes The Sexpert! From penis size to toy care, bar behavior to AIDS awareness, The Sexpert responds to real concerns with uncanny wisdom and a razor wit.

FOR A FREE COPY OF THE COMPLETE MASQUERADE CATALOG, MAIL THIS COUPON TO:
MASQUERADE BOOKS/DEPT X74K
801 SECOND AVENUE, NEW YORK, NY 10017
OR FAX TO 212 986-7355
All transactions are strictly confidential and we never sell, give or trade any customer's name.

NAME _____

ADDRESS _____

CITY _____ STATE _____ ZIP _____

HARD CANDY

RED JORDAN AROBATEAU
Dirty Pictures $6.95/345-7

Another red-hot tale from lesbian sensation Red Jordan Arobateau. *Dirty Pictures* tells the story of a lonely butch tending bar—and the femme she finally calls her own. With the same precision that made *Lucy and Mickey* a breakout debut, Arobateau tells a love story that's the flip-side of "lesbian chic." Not to be missed.

Praise for Arobateau's *Lucy and Mickey*:
"Both deeply philosophical and powerfully erotic.... A necessary reminder to all who blissfully—some may say ignorantly—ride the wave of lesbian chic into the mainstream."
—Heather Findlay, editor-in-chief of *Girlfriends*

LARS EIGHNER
Gay Cosmos $6.95/236-1

A thought-provoking volume from widely acclaimed author Lars Eighner. Eighner has distinguished himself as not only one of America's most accomplished new voices, but a solid-seller—his erotic titles alone have become bestsellers and classics of the genre. Eighner describes *Gay Cosmos* as being a volume of "essays on the place, meaning, and purpose of homosexuality in the Universe, and gay sexuality on human societies."

JAMES COLTON
Todd $6.95/312-0

A remarkably frank novel from an earlier age. With *Todd*, Colton took on the complexities of American race relations, becoming one of the first writers to explore interracial love between two men. Set in 1971, Colton's novel examines the relationship of Todd and Felix, and the ways in which it is threatened by not only the era's politics, but the timeless stumbling block called "the reappearing former lover." Tender and uncompromising, *Todd* takes on issues the gay community struggles with to this day.

The Outward Side $6.95/304-X

The return of a classic tale of one man's struggle with his deepest needs. Marc Lingard, a handsome, respected young minister, finds himself at a crossroads. The homophobic persecution of a local resident unearths Marc's long-repressed memories of a youthful love affair, and he is irrepressibly drawn to his forbidden urges. Originally published two years after Stonewall, Colton's novel helped pave the way for popular gay literature in America. *The Outward Side* promises to enthrall a new generation of gay readers.

STAN LEVENTHAL
Skydiving on Christopher Street $6.95/287-6

"Generosity, evenness, fairness to the reader, sensitivity—these are qualities that most contemporary writers take for granted or overrule with stylistics. In Leventhal's writing they not only stand out, they're positively addictive." —Dennis Cooper

Aside from a hateful job, a hateful apartment, a hateful world and an increasingly hateful lover, life seems, well, all right for the protagonist of Stan Leventhal's latest novel, *Skydiving on Christopher Street*. Having already lost most of his friends to AIDS, how could things get any worse? But things soon do, and he's forced to endure much more before finding a new strength amidst his memories.

1 800 616-HUNG

Dream men are ready, willing and able—to give it to you as *hard* as you need it! No credit cards needed—and no bogus recordings, either! Just the real thing, with a real man who knows what you want. (Must be over 18.) $3.98 per minute.

FELICE PICANO

Men Who Loved Me — $6.95/274-4

In 1966, at the tender-but-bored age of twenty-two, Felice Picano abandoned New York, determined to find true love in Europe. Almost immediately, he encounters Djanko—an exquisite prodigal who sweeps Felice off his feet with the endless string of extravagant parties, glamorous clubs and glittering premieres that made up Rome's *dolce vita*. When the older (slightly) and wiser (vastly) Picano returns to New York at last, he plunges into the city's thriving gay community—experiencing the frenzy and heartbreak that came to define Greenwich Village society in the 1970s. Lush and warm, *Men Who Loved Me* is a matchless portrait of an unforgettable decade.

"Zesty... spiked with adventure and romance.... a distinguished and humorous portrait of a vanished age." —*Publishers Weekly*

"A stunner... captures the free-wheeling spirit of an era."
—*The Advocate*

"Rich, engaging, engrossing... a ravishingly exotic romance."
—*New York Native*

Ambidextrous — $6.95/275-2

"Deftly evokes those placid Eisenhower years of bicycles, boners, and book reports. Makes us remember what it feels like to be a child..."
—*The Advocate*

"Compelling and engrossing... will conjure up memories of everyone's adolescence, straight or gay." —*Out!*

The touching and funny memories of childhood—as only Felice Picano could tell them. Ambi*dextrous* tells the story of Picano's youth in the suburbs of New York during the '50's. Beginning at age eleven, Picano's "memoir in the form of a novel" tells all: home life, school face-offs, the ingenuous sophistications of his first sexual steps. In three years' time, he's had his first gay fling—and is on his way to becoming the writer about whom the *L.A. Herald Examiner* said "[he] can run the length of experience from the lyrical to the lewd without missing a beat." A moving memoir, **Ambidextrous** is sure to reawaken the child's sense of wonder inside everyone.

WILLIAM TALSMAN

The Gaudy Image — $6.95/263-9

Unavailable for years, William Talsman's remarkable pre-Stonewall gay novel returns. Filled with insight into gay life of an earlier period, *The Gaudy Image* stands poised to take its place alongside *Better Angel*, *Quatrefoil* and *The City and the Pillar* as not only an invaluable piece of the community's literary history, but a fascinating, highly-entertaining reading experience.

"To read *The Gaudy Image* now is not simply to enjoy a great novel or an artifact of gay history, it is to see first-hand the very issues of identity and positionality with which gay men and gay culture were struggling in the decades before Stonewall. For what Talsman is dealing with...is the very question of how we conceive ourselves gay."
—from the Introduction by **Michael Bronski**

A RICHARD KASAK BOOK

MICHAEL ROWE
WRITING BELOW THE BELT: Conversations with Erotic Authors

Award-winning journalist Michael Rowe interviewed the best and brightest erotic writers—both those well-known for their work in the field and those just starting out—and presents the collected wisdom in *Writing Below the Belt*. Rowe speaks frankly with cult favorites such as Pat Califia, crossover success stories like John Preston, and up-and-comers Michael Lowenthal and Will Leber. In each revealing conversation, the personal, the political and the just plain prurient collide and complement one another in fascinating ways.

$19.95/363-5

RANDY TUROFF, EDITOR
LESBIAN WORDS: State of the Art

Lesbian Words collects one of the widest assortments of lesbian nonfiction writing in one revealing volume. Dorothy Allison, Jewelle Gomez, Judy Grahn, Eileen Myles, Robin Podolsky and many others are represented by some of their best work, looking at not only the current fashionability the media has brought to the lesbian "image," but important considerations of the lesbian past via historical inquiry and personal recollections. A fascinating, provocative volume, *Lesbian Words* is a virtual primer to contemporary trends in lesbian thought.

$10.95/340-6

EURYDICE
f/32

f/32 has been called "the most controversial and dangerous novel ever written by a woman." With the story of Ela (whose name is a pseudonym for orgasm), Eurydice won the National Fiction competition sponsored by Fiction Collective Two and Illinois State University. A funny, disturbing quest for unity, *f/32* prompted Frederic Tuten to proclaim that "almost any page... redeems us from the anemic writing and banalities we have endured in the past decade of bloodless fiction."

$10.95/350-3

LARRY TOWNSEND
ASK LARRY

Twelve years of Masterful advice from Larry Townsend, the leatherman's long-time confidant and adviser. Starting just before the onslaught of AIDS, Townsend wrote the "Leather Notebook" column for *Drummer* magazine. Now, with *Ask Larry*, readers can avail themselves of Townsend's collected wisdom and contemporary commentary—a careful consideration of the way life has changed in the AIDS era, and the specific ways in which the disease has altered perceptions of once-simple problems.

$12.95/289-2

WILLIAM CARNEY
THE REAL THING

"Carney gives us a good look at the mores and lifestyle of the first generation of gay leathermen. A chilling mystery/romance novel as well."
—Pat Califia

With a new Introduction by Michael Bronski. William Carney's *The Real Thing* has long served as a touchstone in any consideration of gay "edge fiction." First published in 1968, this uncompromising story of New York leathermen received instant acclaim—and in the years since, has become a rare and highly-prized volume to those lucky enough to acquire a copy. Finally, *The Real Thing* returns from exile, ready to thrill a new generation—and reacquaint itself with its original audience.

$10.95/280-9

LOOKING FOR MR. PRESTON

Edited by Laura Antoniou, *Looking for Mr. Preston* includes work by Lars Eighner, Pat Califia, Michael Bronski, Felice Picano, Joan Nestle, Larry Townsend, Andrew Holleran, Michael Lowenthal, and others who contributed interviews, essays and personal reminiscences of John Preston—a man whose career spanned the industry from the early pages of the *Advocate* to national bestseller lists. Preston was the author of over twenty books, including *Franny, the Queen of Provincetown*, and *Mr. Benson*. He also edited the noted *Flesh and the Word* erotic anthologies, *Hometowns*, and *A Member of the Family*. More importantly, Preston became an inspiration, friend and occasionally a mentor to many of today's gay and lesbian authors and editors. Ten percent of the proceeds from sale of the book will go to the AIDS Project of Southern Maine, for whom Preston had served as President of the Board. **$23.95/288-4**

MICHAEL LASSELL
THE HARD WAY

Lassell is a master of the necessary word. In an age of tepid and whining verse, his bawdy and bittersweet songs are like a plunge in cold champagne.

—Paul Monette

Widely anthologized and a staple of gay literary and entertainment publications nationwide, Lassell is regarded as one of the most distinctive and accomplished talents of his generation. As much a chronicle of post-Stonewall gay life as a compendium of a remarkable writer's work, *The Hard Way* is sure to appeal to anyone interested in the state of contemporary writing. **$12.95/231-0**

JOHN PRESTON
MY LIFE AS A PORNOGRAPHER

...essential and enlightening...His sex-positive stand on safer-sex education as the only truly effective AIDS-prevention strategy will certainly not win him any conservative converts, but AIDS activists will be shouting their assent....[My Life as a Pornographer] is a bridge from the sexually liberated 1970s to the more cautious 1990s, and Preston has walked much of that way as a standard-bearer to the cause for equal rights.... —Library Journal
$12.95/135-7

HUSTLING:
A Gentleman's Guide to the Fine Art of Homosexual Prostitution

...valuable insights to many aspects of the world of gay male prostitution. Throughout the book, Preston uses materials gathered from interviews and letters from former and active hustlers, as well as insights gleaned from his own experience as a hustler.... Preston does fulfill his desire to entertain as well as educate. —Lambda Book Report

...fun and highly literary. what more could you expect from such an accomplished activist, author and editor? —Drummer
$12.95/137-3

RUSS KICK
OUTPOSTS:
A Catalog of Rare and Disturbing Alternative Information

A huge, authoritative guide to some of the most offbeat and bizarre publications available today! Russ Kick has tracked down the real McCoy and compiled over five hundred reviews of work penned by political extremists, conspiracy theorists, hallucinogenic pathfinders, sexual explorers, religious iconoclasts and social malcontents. Better yet, each review is followed by ordering information for the many readers sure to want these publications for themselves. No one with a "need to know" can afford to miss this ultra-alternative resource. **$18.95/0202-8**

HUSTLING

A Gentleman's Guide to the Fine Art of Homosexual Prostitution

JOHN PRESTON

SAMUEL R. DELANY
THE MAD MAN
The latest novel from Hugo- and Nebula-winning science fiction writer and critic Delany...reads like a pornographic reflection of Peter Ackroyd's Chatterton *or A.S. Byatt's* Possession.... *The pornographic element... becomes more than simple shock or titillation, though, as Delany develops an insightful dichotomy between [his protagonist]'s two worlds: the one of cerebral philosophy and dry academia, the other of heedless, 'impersonal' obsessive sexual extremism. When these worlds finally collide...the novel achieves a surprisingly satisfying resolution....* —Publishers Weekly
$23.95/193-4

THE MOTION OF LIGHT IN WATER
The first unexpurgated American edition of award-winning author Samuel R. Delany's autobiography covers the early years of one of science fiction's most important voices. Delany paints a compelling picture of New York's East Village in the early '60s—when Bob Dylan took second billing to a certain guitar-toting science fiction writer, W. H. Auden stopped by for dinner, and a walk on the Brooklyn Bridge changed the course of a literary genre. **$12.95/133-0**

ROBERT PATRICK
TEMPLE SLAVE
...you must read this book. It draws such a tragic, and, in a way, noble portrait of Mr. Buono: It leads the reader, almost against his will, into a deep sympathy with this strange man who tried to comfort, to encourage and to feed both the worthy and the worthless... It is impossible not to mourn for this man—impossible not to praise this book. —Quentin Crisp **$12.95/191-8**

LARS EIGHNER
ELEMENTS OF AROUSAL
Critically acclaimed gay writer Lars Eighner—whose *Travels with Lizbeth* was chosen by the *New York Times Book Review* as one of the year's notable titles—develops a guideline for success with one of publishing's best kept secrets: the novice-friendly field of gay erotic writing. In *Elements of Arousal*, Eighner details his craft, providing the reader with sure advice. Eighner's overview of the gay erotic market paints a picture of a diverse array of outlets for a writer's work. Because, after all, writing is what *Elements of Arousal* is about: the application and honing of the writer's craft, which brought Lars Eighner fame with not only the steamy *Bayou Boy*, but the profoundly illuminating *Travels with Lizbeth*. **$12.95/230-2**

PAT CALIFIA
SENSUOUS MAGIC
Clear, succinct and engaging even for the reader for whom S/M isn't the sexual behavior of choice.... Califia's prose is soothing, informative and non-judgmental—she both instructs her reader and explores the territory for them.... Califia is the Dr. Ruth of the alternative sexuality set....
—Lambda Book Report

Renowned erotic pioneer Pat Califia provides this honest, unpretentious peek behind the mask of dominant/submissive sexuality—an adventurous adult world of pleasure too often obscured by ignorance and fear. With her trademark wit and insight, Califia demystifies "the scene" for the novice, explaining the terminology and technique behind many misunderstood sexual practices. The adventurous (or just plain curious) lover won't want to miss this ultimate "how to" volume. One of the best-selling erotic manuals available today. **$12.95/131-4**

ELEMENTS OF AROUSAL

HOW TO WRITE AND SELL GAY MEN'S EROTICA

LARS EIGHNER
Author of *Travels with Lizbeth*

CARO SOLES, EDITOR
MELTDOWN!
An Anthology of Erotic Science Fiction and Dark Fantasy for Gay Men

Editor Caro Soles has put together one of the most explosive, mind-bending collections of gay erotic writing ever published. Soles illustrates the sub-genre with a quick overview of *Meltdown*'s contents:

... From the bleak futuristic world of 'meta-AIDS' where unprotected sex is against the law, to the old fashioned romance of a ghost story; from a transsexual zombie lover, to the alien, hermaphrodite dancer with a secret taste for S/M, this collection covers a lot of territory that is not the usual domain of stories that explore gay sexuality. Here men pursue their tricks and lovers and dream partners through time, space and memory; from the Crusades into the distant future and on to other worlds.... **$12.95/203-5**

MASQUERADE BOOKS

TINY ALICE
The Geek   **$5.95/341-4**

A notorious cult classic. *The Geek* is told from the point of view of, well, a chicken who reports on the various perversities he witnesses as part of a traveling carnival. When a gang of renegade lesbians kidnaps Chicken and his geek, all hell breaks loose. A strange tale, filled with outrageous erotic oddities, that finally returns to print after years of infamy.

"An adventure novel told by a sex-bent male mini-pygmy. This is an accomplishment of which anybody may be proud."
—Philip José Farmer

TITIAN BERESFORD
The Wicked Hand   **$5.95/343-0**

With a special Introduction by *Leg Show*'s Dian Hanson. A collection of fanciful fetishistic tales featuring the absolute subjugation of men by lovely, domineering women. From Japan and Germany to the American heartland—these stories uncover the other side of the "weaker sex."

CHARISSE VAN DER LYN
Sex on the Net   **$5.95/399-6**

Electrifying erotica from one of the Internet's hottest and most widely read authors. Encounters of all kinds—straight, lesbian, dominant/submissive and all sorts of extreme passions—are explored in thrilling detail. Discover what's turning on hackers from coast to coast!

STANLEY CARTEN
Naughty Message   **$5.95/333-3**

Wesley Arthur, a withdrawn computer engineer, discovers a lascivious message on his answering machine. Aroused beyond his wildest dreams by the acts described, Wesley becomes obsessed with tracking down the woman behind the seductive voice. His search takes him through phone sex services, strip clubs and no-tell motels—and finally to his randy reward....

CAROLE REMY
Beauty of the Beast   **$5.95/332-5**

A shocking tell-all, written from the point-of-view of a prize-winning reporter. And what reporting she does! All the secrets of an uninhibited life are revealed, and each lusty tableau is painted in glowing colors. Join in on her scandalous adventures—and reap the rewards of her extensive background in Erotic Affairs!

SIDNEY ST. JAMES

Rive Gauche $5.95/317-1

Decadence and debauchery among the doomed artists in the Latin Quarter, Paris circa 1920. Expatriate bohemians couple with abandon—before eventually abandoning their ambitions amidst the intoxicating temptations waiting to be indulged in every bedroom. Finally, "creative impulse" takes on a whole new meaning for each lusty eccentric!

J. P. KANSAS

Andrea at the Center $5.95/324-4

Kidnapped! Lithe and lovely young Andrea is, without warning, whisked away to a distant retreat. Gradually, she is introduced to the ways of the Center, and soon becomes quite friendly with its other inhabitants—all of whom are learning to abandon all restraint! A big, brawling tale of total submission.

SARA H. FRENCH

Master of Timberland $5.95/327-9

"Welcome to Timberland Resort," he began. "We are delighted that you have come to serve us. And…be assured that we will require service of you in the strictest sense. Our discipline is the most demanding in the world. You will be trained here by the best. And now your new Masters will make their choices." A tale of sexual slavery at the ultimate paradise resort. One of our runaway bestsellers.

PAUL LITTLE

The Prisoner $5.95/330-9

Judge Black has built a secret room below a penitentiary, where he sentences the prisoners to hours of exhibition and torment while his friends watch. Judge Black's House of Corrections is equipped with one purpose in mind: to administer his own brand of rough justice!

All the Way $4.95/3023-7

Two excruciating novels from Paul Little in one hot volume! *Going All the Way* features an unhappy man who tries to purge himself of the memory of his lover with a series of quirky and uninhibited lovers. *Pushover* tells the story of a serial spanker and his celebrated exploits. These stories combine to make one of Little's most perfectly debauched titles.

Slave Island $4.95/3006-7

Lord Philbrock, a sadistic genius, has built a hidden paradise where captive females are forced into slavery. Cruise ships are waylaid, and the unsuspecting passengers put through Lord Philbrock's training. They are trained to accommodate the most bizarre sexual cravings of the rich, the famous, the pampered, and the perverted.

Chinese Justice $4.95/153-5

The notorious Paul Little indulges his penchant for discipline in these wild tales. *Chinese Justice* is already a classic—the story of the excruciating pleasures and delicious punishments inflicted on foreigners under the tyrannical leaders of the Boxer Rebellion.

TITIAN BERESFORD

Cinderella $4.95/024-5

A magical exploration of the full erotic potential of this fairy tale. Titian Beresford (*Nina Foxton, Judith Boston*) triumphs again with castle dungeons and tightly corseted ladies-in-waiting, naughty viscounts and impossibly cruel masturbatrixes—nearly every conceivable method of erotic torture is explored and described in lush, vivid detail. A fetishist's dream!

MASQUERADE

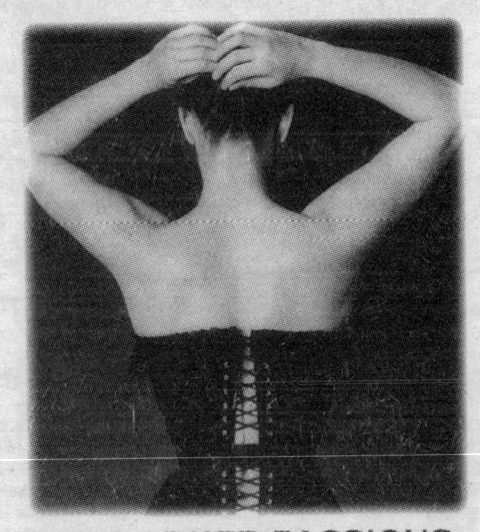

THE DARKER PASSIONS:
THE FALL OF THE HOUSE OF USHER

AMARANTHA KNIGHT

CHARLOTTE ROSE

A Dangerous Day $5.95/293-0
A new volume from the best-selling author who brought you the sensational *Women at Work* and *The Doctor Is In*. And if you thought the high-powered entanglements of her previous books were risky, wait until Rose takes you on a journey through the thrills of one dangerous day! A woman learns to let go—with the help of a mysterious and sexy stranger, who takes her places she has never been....

AMARANTHA KNIGHT

The Darker Passions: Dracula $5.95/326-0
From the realm of legend comes the grand beast of Eros, the famed and dreaded seducer and defiler of innocence. His name is Dracula, and no virgin is protected from his unspeakable ravishments. One by one he brings his victims to the ecstasy that will make them his forever. An acclaimed modern classic, and the first of Knight's "Darker Passions."

The Darker Passions: The Fall of the House of Usher $5.95/313-9
Two weary travelers arrive at the Usher home—a gloomy manse wherein they will find themselves faced with the dark secrets of desire. The Master and Mistress of the house indulge in every conceivable form of decadence, and are intent on initiating their guests into the many pleasures to be found in utter submission. But something is not quite right in the House of Usher, and the foundation of its dynasty begins to crack....

The Darker Passions: Dr. Jekyll and Mr. Hyde $5.95/227-2
It is a classic story, one of incredible, frightening transformations achieved through mysterious experiments. Now, Amarantha Knight—author of the popular erotic retelling of the Dracula legend—explores the steamy possibilities of a tale where no one is quite who they seem.

SARAH JACKSON

Sanctuary $5.95/318-X
Tales from the Middle Ages. *Sanctuary* explores both the unspeakable debauchery of court life and the unimaginable privations of monastic solitude, leading the voracious and the virtuous on a collision course that brings history to throbbing life. Bored royals and yearning clerics start fires sure to bring light to the darkest of ages.

ALIZARIN LAKE

The Instruments of the Passion $4.95/3010-5
All that remains is the diary of a young initiate, detailing the rituals of a mysterious cult institution known only as "Rossiter." Behind sinister walls, a beautiful woman performs an unending drama of pain and humiliation. Will she ever be satisfied...?

ANONYMOUS

School Days in Paris $5.95/325-2
A delicious duo of erotic awakenings. The rapturous chronicles of a well-spent youth! Few Universities provide the profound and pleasurable lessons one learns in after-hours study—particularly if one is young and bursting with promise, and lucky enough to have Paris as a playground.

Jennifer III $5.95/292-2
The further adventures of erotica's most daring heroine. Jennifer, the quintessential beautiful blonde, has a photographer's eye for detail—particularly details of the masculine variety! Jennifer lets nothing stand between her and her goal: total pleasure through sensual abandon.

Man With a Maid $4.95/307-4
Over 80,000 copies in print! A classic of its genre, *Man with a Maid* tells an outrageous tale of desire, revenge, and submission.

Man With a Maid II $4.95/3071-7
Jack's back! With the assistance of the perverse Alice, he embarks again on a trip through every erotic extreme. Jack leaves no one unsatisfied—least of all, himself, and Alice is always certain to outdo herself in her capacity to corrupt and control. An incendiary sequel!

Man With a Maid: The Conclusion $4.95/3013-X
The final chapter in this saga of lust that has thrilled readers for decades. The adulterous woman who is corrected with enthusiasm and the clumsy maid who receives grueling guidance are just two who benefit from these lessons!

The Complete Erotic Reader $4.95/3063-6
The very best in erotic writing together in a wicked collection sure to stimulate even the most jaded and "sophisticated" palates.

RHINOCEROS BOOKS

No Other Tribute — Edited by Laura Antoniou
A collection of stories sure to challenge Political Correctness in a way few have before, with tales of women kept in bondage to their lovers by their deepest passions. Love pushes these women beyond acceptable limits, rendering them helpless to deny the men and women they adore. Laura Antoniou brings together the most provocative women's writing in this companion volume to *By Her Subdued*. **$6.95/294-9**

Flesh Fantastic — Edited by Amarantha Knight
Humans have long toyed with the idea of "playing God": creating life from nothingness, bringing Life to the inanimate. Now Amarantha Knight, author of the "Darker Passions" series, collects the very best stories exploring not only the allure of Creation, but the lust that may follow.... **$6.96/352-X**

Venus in Furs — Leopold von Sacher-Masoch
This classic 19th century novel is the first uncompromising exploration of the dominant/submissive relationship in literature. The alliance of Severin and Wanda epitomizes Sacher-Masoch's obsession with a cruel, controlling goddess and the urges that drive the man held in her thrall. **$6.95/3089-X**

The Loving Dominant — John Warren
"Mentor"—as the author is known on the scene—is a longtime player in the dominance/submission scene, and he guides readers through this rarely seen world, and offers clear-eyed advice guaranteed to enlighten the most jaded erotic explorers. Mentor reveals the hidden basis of the D/S relationship: the care, trust and love between partners. **$6.95/218-3**

Season of the Witch — Jean Stine
He committed an unforgivable crime, and and pays for it in ways that he never imagined. A rapist undergoes the ultimate punishment— transformation into the woman who was his target... **$6.95/268-X**

GARY BOWEN

Diary of a Vampire $5.95/331-7
"Gifted with a darkly sensual vision and a fresh voice, [Bowen] is a writer to watch out for."
—Cecilia Tan

The chilling, arousing, and ultimately moving memoirs of an undead—but all too human—soul. Rafael, a red-blooded male with an insatiable hunger for same, is the perfect antidote to the effete malcontents haunting bookstores today. A bold and brilliant vision, firmly rooted in past *and* present.

VENUS IN FURS
AND SELECTED LETTERS

"This 19th century classic re-examines what is at stake in the contract between the submissive and the dominant."
—Graham Caveney, *City Limits*

LEOPOLD VON SACHER-MASOCH

ANDREI CODRESCU

The Repentance of Lorraine $6.95/329-5

"His command of language is superb, his writing beautifully original, and his insights piercing." —*Harper's Magazine*

"One of our most prodigiously talented and magical writers."
—*New York Times Book Review*

From one of America's foremost writers and social commentators comes an early erotic romp. Hot on the heels of Codrescu's latest novel (*The Blood Countess*) comes the reissue of one of his first—the enchanting *Repentance of Lorraine*.

PHILIP JOSÉ FARMER

Flesh $6.95/303-1

One of Farmer's most infamous science fiction yarns. Space Commander Stagg explored the galaxies for 800 years, and could only hope that he would be welcomed home by an adoring—or at least *appreciative*—public. And upon his return, the hero Stagg is made the centerpiece of an incredible public ritual—one that will repeatedly take him to the heights of ecstasy, and inexorably drag him toward the depths of hell.

A Feast Unknown $6.95/276-0

"Sprawling, brawling, shocking, suspenseful, hilarious..."
—Theodore Sturgeon

Farmer's supreme anti-hero returns. *A Feast Unknown* begins in 1968, with Lord Grandrith's stunning statement: "I was conceived and born in 1888. Jack the Ripper was my father." Slowly, Lord Grandrith—armed with this belief—tells the story of his remarkable and unbridled life. Beginning with his discovery of the secret of immortality, Grandrith's tale proves him no raving lunatic—but something far more bizarre....

MICHAEL PERKINS

The Secret Record: Modern Erotic Literature $6.95/3039-3

Perkins, a renowned author and critic of sexually explicit fiction, surveys the field with authority and unique insight. Updated and revised to include the latest trends, tastes, and developments in this much-misunderstood genre.

GRANT ANTREWS

Submissions $6.95/207-8

Another stunning, sensitive tale from the author of *My Darling Dominatrix*. Once again, Antrews portrays the very special elements of the dominant/submissive relationship with restraint—this time with the story of a lonely man, a winning lottery ticket, and a demanding dominatrix.

SARA ADAMSON

"Ms. Adamson's friendly, conversational writing style perfectly couches what to some will be shocking material. Ms. Adamson creates a wonderfully diverse world of lesbian, gay, straight, bi and transgendered characters, all mixing delightfully in the melting pot of sadomasochism and planting the genre more firmly in the culture at large. I for one am cheering her on!" —Kate Bornstein

The Trainer $6.95/249-3

The long-awaited conclusion of Adamson's stunning Marketplace Trilogy! The ultimate underground sexual realm includes not only willing slaves, but the exquisite and demanding trainers who take submissives firmly in hand. And it is now the time for these mentors to lay bare the desires that compelled them to become the ultimate figures of erotic authority.

The Slave $6.95/173-X
The second volume in the "Marketplace" trilogy. *The Slave* covers the experience of one exceptionally talented submissive who longs to join the ranks of those who have proven themselves worthy of entry into the Marketplace. But the price, while delicious, is staggeringly high....

The Marketplace $6.95/3096-2
"Merchandise does not come easily to the Marketplace.... They haunt the clubs and the organizations, their need so real and desperate that they exude sensual tension when they glide through the crowds. Some of them are so ripe that they intimidate the poseurs, the weekend sadists and the furtive dilettantes who are so endemic to that world. And they never stop asking where we are found..."

ROSEBUD BOOKS

The Rosebud Reader $5.95/319-8
Rosebud Books—the hottest-selling line of lesbian erotica available—here collects the very best of the best. Rosebud has contributed greatly to the burgeoning genre of lesbian erotica—to the point that authors like Lindsay Welsh, Aarona Griffin and Valentina Cilescu are among the hottest and most closely watched names in lesbian and gay publishing. Here are the finest moments from Rosebud's contemporary classics.

LINDSAY WELSH

Provincetown Summer $5.95/362-7
"These tales are extremely enjoyable...reading may be interrupted by increased passion."
—*Perception*

This completely original collection is devoted exclusively to white-hot desire between women. From the casual encounters of women on the prowl to the enduring erotic bonds between old lovers, the women of *Provincetown Summer* will set your senses on fire! A nationally best-selling title.

A Victorian Romance $5.95/365-1
Lust-letters from the road. A young Englishwoman realizes her dream—a trip abroad under the guidance of her eccentric maiden aunt. Soon the young but blossoming Elaine comes to discover her own sexual talents, as a hot-blooded Parisian named Madelaine takes her Sapphic education in hand.

A Circle of Friends $4.95/250-7
The author of the nationally best-selling *Provincetown Summer* returns with the story of a remarkable group of women. Slowly, the women pair off to explore all the possibilities of lesbian passion, until finally it seems that there is nothing and no one they have not dabbled in.

EDITED BY LAURA ANTONIOU

"...a great new collection of fiction by and about SM dykes."
—*SKIN TWO*

Leatherwomen $4.95/3095-4
A groundbreaking anthology. These fantasies, from the pens of new or emerging authors, break every rule imposed on women's fantasies. The hottest stories from some of today's newest writers make this an unforgettable exploration of the female libido.

Leatherwomen II $4.95/229-9
Once again, Laura Antoniou turned a discerning eye to the writing of women on the edge—resulting in a second collection sure to ignite libidinal flames in any reader. Leave taboos behind, and be ready to speak the unspeakable—because these Leatherwomen know no limits...

MISTRESS MINE

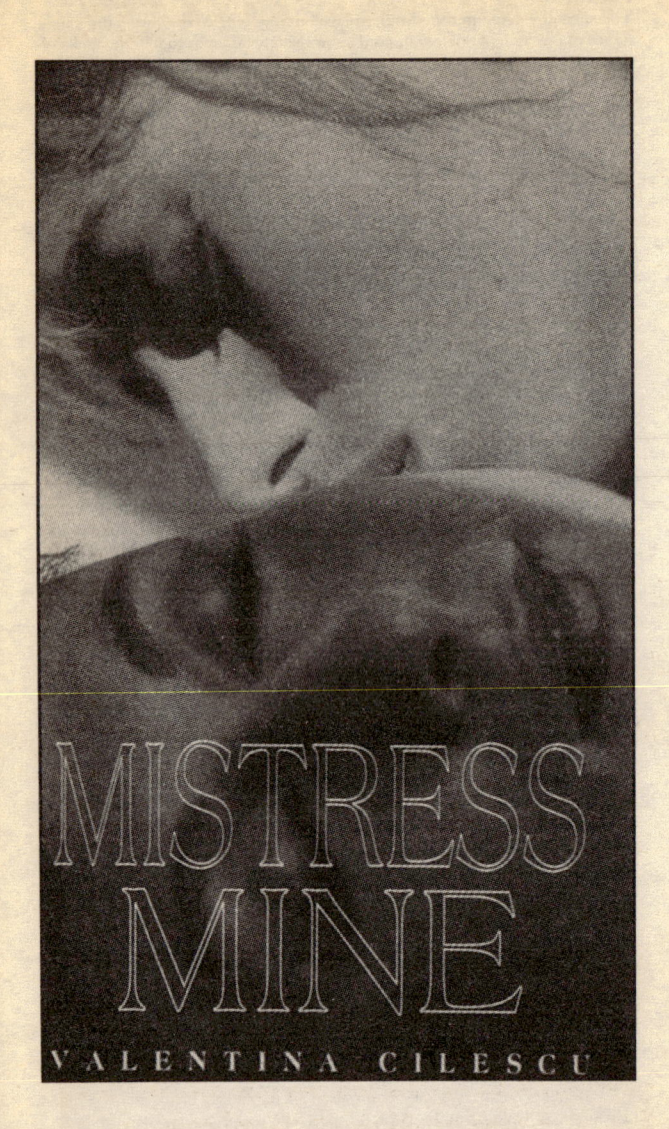

VALENTINA CILESCU

VALENTINA CILESCU
Mistress Mine $4.95/109-8
Sophia Cranleigh sits in prison, accused of authoring the "obscene" *Mistress Mine*. She is offered salvation—with the condition that she first relate her lurid life story. For Sophia has led no ordinary life, but has slaved and suffered—deliciously—under the hand of the notorious Mistress Malin. Sophia tells her story, never imagining the way in which she'd be repaid for her honesty....

ELIZABETH OLIVER
Pagan Dreams $5.95/295-7
Cassidy and Samantha plan a quiet vacation at a secluded bed-and-breakfast, hoping for a little personal time alone. Their hostess, however, has different plans. The lovers are plunged into a shadowy world of dungeons and pagan rites, as the merciless Anastasia steals Samantha for her own. B&B—B&D-style!

ALISON TYLER
The Blue Rose $5.95/335-X
The tale of a modern sorority—fashioned after a Victorian girls' school. Ignited to the heights of passion by erotic tales of the Victorian age, a group of lusty young women are encouraged to act out their forbidden fantasies—all under the tutelage of Mistresses Emily and Justine, two avid practitioners of hard-core discipline!

E-mail us! MasqBks@aol.com

ORDERING IS EASY!

MC/VISA orders can be placed by calling our toll-free number

PHONE 800 375-2356/FAX 212 986-7355

or mail the coupon below to:

MASQUERADE BOOKS
DEPT. X74A, 801 SECOND AVENUE, NY, NY 10017

BUY ANY FOUR BOOKS AND CHOOSE ONE ADDITIONAL BOOK, OF EQUAL OR LESSER VALUE, AS YOUR FREE GIFT.

QTY.	TITLE	NO.	PRICE
			FREE
			FREE

X74A

SUBTOTAL

POSTAGE and HANDLING

We Never Sell, Give or Trade Any Customer's Name.

TOTAL

In the U.S., please add $1.50 for the first book and 75¢ for each additional book; in Canada, add $2.00 for the first book and $1.25 for each additional book. Foreign countries: add $4.00 for the first book and $2.00 for each additional book. No C.O.D. orders. Please make all checks payable to Masquerade Books. Payable in U.S. currency only. New York state residents add $8^{1/4}$% sales tax. Please allow 4-6 weeks delivery.

NAME _____

ADDRESS _____

CITY _____ STATE _____ ZIP _____

TEL ( ) _____

PAYMENT: ☐ CHECK ☐ MONEY ORDER ☐ VISA ☐ MC

CARD NO. _____ EXP. DATE _____